ALLIANCE FORCES

OUTER RIM COMMAND, TATOOINE PATROL

INCIDENT REPORT 39:3:22

Seized Starship *Slave I* (S011-261MAC-TR17, operator: Fett, Boba) located in geosynchronous Tatooine orbit. Among items found in cockpit was one (1) volume, presumably bound by Boba Fett. Returned to GCSF, where its contents were examined prior to archiving. Starship towed to impound lot GRA-9-09 (Grakouine central yards).

CONTENTS OF BOOK:

- Fett's *Bounty Hunters Guild Handbook*. Includes handwritten comments from B. Fett and the bounty hunters Greedo, Bossk, and Dengar. And General Solo
- *Ba'jurne Kyr'tsad Mando'ad*, a Death Watch manifesto. Includes handwritten comments from B. Fett, J. Fett, Aurra Sing, and the Weequay pirate Honda Ohnaka.

NOTES:

Intelligence value of annotations still unknown.
Jango Fett's comments appear directed to Boba Fett, some of whose comments were intended for his daughter, Ailyn Vel.

Capt. Noan Jeraddi
Capt. Noan Jeraddi

Lt Tepra Tseelit
Lt. Tepra Tseelit

FROM THE FILES OF BOBA FETT

THE BOUNTY HUNTERS GUILD HANDBOOK

DENGAR GAVE ME THIS COPY OF THE HANDBOOK. BOSSK AND GREEDO MUST HAVE OWNED IT BEFORE HIM. THEIR NOTES ARE WRITTEN THROUGHOUT. KNOWING WHAT THE GUILD IS UP TO AND HOW THEY DO BUSINESS HAS PROVEN USEFUL TO ME. BOBA

UPDATED IMPERIAL EDITION

Cradossk knows me so well! — Greedo

Greetings from the Head of the Bounty Hunters Guild.

No matter where you come from or what kind of life you've led, I already know a few things about you. As good as you are at handling a weapon or a vehicle, you are determined to improve your skills. You get restless if you stay on any world for too long. You know many laws in numerous star systems, but you have no intention of using that knowledge in a courtroom. You are inquisitive by nature, yet have a cautious distrust of most sentient life forms. If time allows, you won't enter a building until after you've discreetly inspected every exit. You are not averse to fighting to get what you need. You have little respect for those who can't defend themselves, but you respect their economic worth if they become subjects of bounties. You take satisfaction in doing things right. You take pride in the way you earn your money.

How do I know these things? Because we think alike. Our profession binds us as comrades in arms.

We bounty hunters appreciate the value of information and technical know-how. And no matter how antisocial you may feel in general, you know there are disadvantages to working entirely on your own. You need connections. To stay alive and get the job done, you sometimes require support and allies to watch your back. In other words, you need the Bounty Hunters Guild, and the Guild needs you.

For nearly a thousand years, the Bounty Hunters Guild Handbook has kept Guild members alive and informed. This updated edition features insights from master hunters and overviews of trade tools that have only been recently introduced to the market. It also includes the most current data about the hunting protocols in Imperial space, enabling you to carry out your work in full compliance with the Imperial Office of Criminal Investigations.

You have the book. The hunt awaits. Now get to work!

Cradossk

HEAD OF THE BOUNTY HUNTERS GUILD

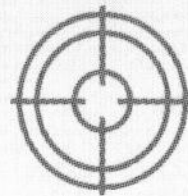

Ontondon's text hasn't changed fo
at least two editions.
— Dengar

THE BASICS

BY GLEED ONTONDON, DEPUTY CHIEF EXECUTIVE, BOUNTY HUNTERS GUILD COUNCIL

Thanks to countless holo-thrillers, the popular opinion of bounty hunters is that we're cold, calculating individuals who measure a person's worth by the price on his head. Most civilians, and even many governmental officials, regard us as greedy, trigger-happy opportunists. They have even been known to call us scum.

Call *me* scum and see what happens.
– Bossk

We know the truth about who we are and what we do.

WHAT BOUNTY HUNTERS DO

We have the toughest job in the galaxy. We pursue the most dangerous criminals and killers after others have failed and when no one else dares. Few people appreciate that ours is a necessary job, a job that *someone* has to do. While others cringe and whimper in weakness and indecision, we're the ones who get things done.

But every bounty hunter has to start sometime, and I understand that you're new and don't know all the ins and outs of the trade. Here's how the job works. Someone commits a crime. The Empire, a local government, a corporation, or an individual issues a notification to the Bounty Hunters Guild, offering a reward for the capture or execution of the criminal. The entity that issues the notification is known as the *originator*. The criminal who is the subject of the notification is called the *acquisition*. The reward, of course, is the *bounty*.

The originator usually issues a bounty notification because the local or regional law-enforcement services are unable or unwilling to tackle the challenge on their own. After the notification arrives at a Bounty Hunters Guild office, a Guild *contractor* determines which hunter will track down and apprehend the acquisition. The hunter cannot refuse an assignment from the Guild contractor.

All these rules! – Greedo

If he'd paid attention to the rules, he might have lived longer. – Dengar

Contractors review notifications. It's their job, not yours.

The hunter must capture and deliver the acquisition—or the remains or other evidence of the acquisition's death—to a designated person, corporation, or location, known as the *receiver*. The bounty is typically paid in credits, either hard cash or a direct transfer to the Bounty Hunters Guild. Sounds easy, doesn't it?

Sure, it's easy. Like playing Count My Teeth with a rancor.

I played that game once. I have the rancor tooth to prove it. – Bossk

If the job were easy, anyone could do it. But you're not just anyone. You're a member of the Guild.

Anyone can play it with a dead rancor. – Dengar

MISCONCEPTIONS ABOUT BOUNTY HUNTERS

Now that we've covered the basics of the job, let's straighten out some misconceptions about what we do for a living.

There's nothing wrong with "mere" personal gain. - Bossk

Do bounty hunters kill for money? Yes, but not indiscriminately, and not merely for personal gain. Members of the Bounty Hunters Guild accept rewards for killing *criminals*, and only when a lawfully issued bounty notification requires the acquisition dead, and a percentage of the bounty goes to the Guild.

Are bounty hunters murderers? No. Murderers kill unlawfully.

Are bounty hunters assassins? No. Assassins typically target specific individuals for political or religious reasons, and do not necessarily profit from the killing. Most so-called professional assassins have no compunction about accepting money to kill innocent people.

Do bounty hunters kill innocent people? Never intentionally, and not without consequence. Members of the Bounty Hunters Guild make every effort to ensure the safety of innocent life-forms and prevent collateral damage. When accidents occur, the Guild's legal and insurance departments work with other authorities to compensate innocents and their relatives for any specified loss, damage, illness, and death. The Guild is in the business of stopping criminals, not harming innocents. The Guild is not responsible, however, for injuries, deaths, or damage caused by acquisitions during a hunt.

Do Imperial laws apply to bounty hunters? Yes. Again, bounty hunters are law-enforcement officers, and Guild hunters are expected to comply with and uphold Imperial laws, as well as the laws of the Bounty Hunters Guild. Stiff fines, prison sentences, forced labor camps, and death are among the possible sentences for hunters who break laws.

Are bounty hunters mercenaries? Absolutely not. Mercenaries are freelance soldiers hired to serve in foreign armies. Bounty hunters have little regard for anyone whose allegiance is for sale.

Are all bounty hunters members of the Bounty Hunters Guild? No. Unfortunately for them, some hunters prefer to work independently. They don't last long.

Do bounty hunters compete with each other? Not if they're members of the Bounty Hunters Guild or an affiliate guild. Because Guild contractors assign Guild hunters to pursue specific bounties, Guild hunters seldom cross paths, but when they do, they respect each other as allies. As for non-Guild hunters, if they interfere with an authorized Guild hunt, the Guild will make sure they never compete again. THE BEST DON'T NEED BACKUP. BOBA

…ssk competes with everyone. – Dengar

Do bounty hunters do freelance work? Guild hunters are allowed to pursue any sanctioned bounties with the provision that their work for the Guild comes first and that the Guild receives a percentage of their non-Guild earnings. But remember that "freelance" is not an excuse for bad behavior. You are not a hired gun. You are a bounty hunter, a licensed law-enforcement officer, and don't let anyone tell you different. You are not a wage slave, and you cannot be bought.

Got that? Good.

Kill if the job requires it, but always stay in control. And never go outside the terms of the contract.

BECOMING A BOUNTY HUNTER

BY ARACK "DEADEYE" DOSTRYT,
DIRECTOR OF RECRUITING

So you want to be a bounty hunter. Understand this: as long as your skills are sharp, no one will judge your motivations.

But the galaxy doesn't view hunters kindly. The headline chasers on the HoloNet claim we're a pack of armored outlaws. Jealous law officers badmouth us because we do their jobs better than they do. And the kids playing dress-up by freelancing as "independent hunters" make the whole profession look like a bunch of sloppy amateurs.

So think hard before you make it your career. In the Bounty Hunters Guild we've seen it all. Trust me, your reasons aren't unique. Let me take a few stabs at what brings you here:

- **The family business.** Father, mother, cousin, mentor. Someone walked the path of the hunter. You want to honor their memory.

I'd like to honor my father's corpse! - Bossk

- **The vendetta.** Somebody wronged you, so you want to become a hunter and dish out payback. There's nothing wrong with revenge, but don't let it interfere with your work. Handle your personal problems on your own time. Bounty hunting is a business.

Payback. You're playing my song. – Dengar.

- **The hunting culture.** Ever wonder why the Guild attracts so many Rodians? It's in their blood. Bounty hunters are the Rodian heroes and gods, and Rodians write eight-hour operas about the art of the hunt. Same thing for Trandoshans, minus the operas. The Gand celebrate the hunt, too, as do the Togorians. Even the

Corellians have their hunting traditions, with the masked "Thief-Takers" fighting bandit kings.

- **The noble intention.** Some hunters are true believers. They'll talk until your eyes dry out, going on and on about how we keep the peace. They might be irritating, but they're not wrong. We stop killers before they strike again, and we force fugitives to face justice. And we're *great* at it.
- **The practical motivation.** Everybody needs money, right? There's no shame in being well paid for a dangerous job. Maybe you send your pay back home to feed your mate's new litter of kits, or maybe you blow it all on Savareen brandy. It makes no difference to your Guildmates. You made it, you decide how to spend it.
- **The quirk.** In the Guild, oddballs are the norm, not the exception. And may the Edge bless us for harboring such a stable of extraordinary freaks. Take Tyrn Jiton, so precise with a blaster rifle he only needs to fire it once, but so reckless at gambling that he's lost seven fortunes. Or Count Dojarat of Prospera Jang, the gentleman adventurer who lets his marks go free if they beat him at boxing. Then there's Zalli the Zelosian, a techhunter who tests a new invention every time she hits the field, but only because she's superstitious about using the same weapon twice.

I saw Jiton blow a sabacc game in Mos Eisley. – Greedo

The Ualaq from Prospera Jang has a devastating left.

This isn't the Imperial stormtrooper corps. You've never fit in? *You'll fit right in.*

REQUIREMENTS FOR JOINING THE BOUNTY HUNTERS GUILD

As a Guild hunter you're going to attract attention. And anybody who's not too scared will pipe up and start asking questions. Dirty alley kids who like the painted flames on your armor. Dumb farmers who shoot womp rats with slugthrowers and think they can handle a real hunt. Independent hunters who are desperate for the chance to do what you did and move up from the scrub leagues. They'll all blink at you with big eyes, whistle at your blaster rifle, and ask where they can go to sign up with the Bounty Hunters Guild. And that's when you tell them to go to the Void.

Tell them to keep aiming low if they want to stay alive. Tell them to join the Imperial Army if they're so hot on wearing armor. No one who has the will to become a hunter will hear those words and run home crying. Standards for joining the Guild are high. They should be, especially now that the Empire has cracked down on fringe worlds and sent so many homeless Rimmers knocking on our door.

Quoting from BHG administrative 2-49: *Prerequisites, Conduct, and Regulations*:

1. Each candidate for membership in the Bounty Hunters Guild must be sponsored by at least one existing member of the Bounty Hunters Guild.

2. Each candidate for membership in the Bounty Hunters Guild must pay an evaluation fee of 750 credits.

3. Each candidate for membership in the Bounty Hunters Guild must have a minimum of five (5) confirmed captures, with bounty payouts totaling at least 20,000 credits.

4. Each candidate for membership in the Bounty Hunters Guild must survive the initiation test.

The initiation was rough! – Greedo

The initiation was a joke. -Bossk

That last one's the kicker. For my initiation I had to wrestle Cradossk, and I only lost a chunk of my shoulder. But that clause—the Fighting Fourth—is the one that will scare off the scrubs.

If you face an initiation like mine, you'll probably pass as long as you don't embarrass yourself. (Or die, which is plenty embarrassing.) Show some guts and the Guild won't care if you're short or you're built like a stick. The Guild wants *rrakktorr*, as the Wookiees call it. The heart of a hunter.

Wookiee heart is delicious. - Bossk

THE BOX IS MOBILE AT LAST REPORT. BWAHL THE HUTT HAS GOT IT ON A TOUR OF KAJIDIC STRONGHOLDS, TORTURING ENEMIES FOR ENTERTAINMENT. BoBA

Sure, some Guild initiations are as tough as you've heard. The Box is no rumor. It's a sealed cubic arena at the Guildhouse on Serenno, built by the psychotic Phindian inventor Moralo Eval during the Clone Wars. It's been chewing up rookie hunters ever since.

The Box. Six enter, one leaves and joins the Guild.

What they like to do on Serenno is toss a half-dozen fresh-meat hopefuls into the Box at the same time, with a guaranteed membership to the first to crawl back out. What's in there? Whatever the programmers cook up. The Box is a challenge simulator made of shifting panels, and behind those panels is lots and lots of pain in one form or another.

I'm not saying you'll die inside the Box. Of course, I'm not saying you won't, either. All I know is that on my last run out that way, the resupply crates stacked next to the maintenance hatch were labeled "DIOXIS GAS," "INCENDIARY PROPELLANT," and "INDUSTRIAL CUTTING LASERS."

MEMBERSHIP EXCEPTIONS

There's a hard way and an easy way to do anything, and one shortcut to Guild membership is membership in an affiliate bounty hunting guild. (See "Affiliate Bounty Hunter Guilds," p. 116.) Once you're in with a qualifying affiliate, you're in with the Bounty Hunters Guild automatically, but the rest of us know what's really up.

Say you're in House Benelex. That means you've never had to go through an initiation, but you did have to shell out a pricier evaluation fee of 2,000 credits. Benelex hunters have always had more money than guts, so congratulations on proving it yet again. Or say you're in House Renliss, and you had to pass the extra requirement of being female. Lady Gratina has her own traditions to uphold.

And then there's the Golden Exception. Guilds don't usually admit this, but it's true for all of them, and here it is: *If the boss wants you in, you're in.*

My father never handed me anything! - Bossk

Maybe you're a legacy to fill mama's or papa's boots, or maybe you're good at hunting one particular species of critter and the boss just expanded operations into a sector that's crawling with them. Maybe you've got dirt on the boss. Maybe you beat him at sabacc and he's squaring a debt.

Talk about having a chip on yo shoulder. – Dengar

Doesn't really matter, does it? What matters is your skill, how you carry yourself, and whether you follow the Bounty Hunters' Creed. And whether you can keep your head. (And all your other parts.) Once you're a member, your Guildmates will give you more grief than you can imagine. But you're among the elite.

Republics may fall, empires may rise. But the Bounty Hunters Guild stands strong.

omeday I'll
ave a den
like this.
– Greedo

That wamp
on the wa
was my kil
- Bossk

Recreational games offer excellent opportunities to get to know your fellow Guild members.

THE CREED AND THE CODES

THE BOUNTY HUNTERS' CREED

All bounty hunters know the Creed, and the real ones actually follow it. But the Bounty Hunters Guild *wrote* it. Fail to follow any point of the Creed and you won't be one of us for long.

The Creed's six tenets are what separate bounty hunters from bodyguards, mercenaries, and thugs. It draws authority not from outside institutions of law, but from us, its backers.

The First Tenet: People Don't Have Bounties, Only Acquisitions Have Bounties. Think on this—when a person gets a price on his head, he's *no longer a person*. He's an acquisition. He's hard merchandise. That's what moral crusaders don't understand about hunters. We're not the villains and we didn't post the bounty. The target did the bad stuff. You're not the target's judge, or his conscience, or his mother. You're an agent of justice who will drag him in for what he did.

The Second Tenet: Capture By Design, Kill By Necessity. Wanted postings often say Dead or Alive, and sometimes they just say Dead. So you can kill when the job gives you that flexibility. But if you kill outside those parameters, you're just an assassin.

Now, sometimes captures turn into kills. Shootouts end badly, or acquisitions choose suicide over a Hutt prison. Those are bad outcomes, and they're something you should always avoid. They make you look bad, and that makes *us* look bad.

In some Rim cantinas, the walls are blanketed with wanted posters.

The Third Tenet: No Hunter Shall Slay Another Hunter. If the Creed lowers bounty targets to the level of merchandise, it elevates bounty hunters to the status of professionals. You *try* not to kill an acquisition, unless it's part of the job. You *must* not kill a hunter, no matter what.

Hunting is a competitive business, so this needs to be spelled out again and again, using short words. Listen up. There might be dozens of independent hunters working the same job you are. Silencing one of them with a shot to the helmet would make it easier for you to nab the bounty free and clear. But you're not going to do it. Because even scrub hunters are still hunters.

On the other hand, a hunter who's been drummed out of our fellowship by a lodgment verdict is a hunter no more. On them, it's open season.

Boba Fett doesn't obey this one! — Greedo

The Fourth Tenet: No Hunter Shall Interfere with Another's Hunt. If you thought the third tenet was tough to swallow, this one will really burn your gut. But it's no mystery why it's needed. Bounty hunting is a careful art. It can take months of prep to locate a target's hidey-hole. Don't dishonor a fellow hunter by kicking over his cards, for Edge's sake. We get enough of that from chuff-sucking hunt saboteurs.

OLD WORDS FROM DEAD OWARD. BOBA

The Fifth Tenet: In the Hunt, One Captures *or* Kills, Never Both. None of that "killed while trying to escape" stuff, said with a wink and a smirk, which the Empire does so well. If you capture live, you deliver live. Hunters aren't murderers.

The Sixth Tenet: No Hunter Shall Refuse Aid to Another Hunter. It's written into the Creed that a hunter must help out a rival if asked, and any real hunter will honor that directive. Nobody expects your generosity to go unrewarded, however. If you're asked to help another hunter capture a big bruiser like an Esoomian, you can expect to take ten to forty percent of the bounty (depending on how much work your new partner put into the setup). That keeps things fair and profitable. Just make sure you agree on the split *before* the takedown.

My Tenet: Get in my way and you're dead. - Bossk

Coordinated takedowns can bag even the biggest brutes. Don't forget to share.

GUILD REGULATIONS

The Guild is strong because its members are strong. And how does the Guild *keep you* strong? How does it offer you Guildhouse training, or a starship repair yard, or an armorer's office where you can sign out a jet pack? You've got it: dues.

PLUS HIDDEN FEES, UPKEEP FEES, AND PENALTIES. NEW GUILD HUNTERS ARE NERFS WAITING FOR THE FLEECING. BOBA

If you take advantage of the Guild's benefits, it's only right that you give back some coin. It costs 2,000 credits annually to keep your spot in the Bounty Hunters Guild, and even more if you also claim membership in an affiliate guild.

But the Bounty Hunters Guild can't live on dues alone. The biggest piece of the Guild's annual intake is what it collects from actual bounties. Guild Administration Points calculate the amount you owe out of each of your bounties, and this contractual gap is levied no matter what you *think* you deserve. Nobody cares how many kicks to the head you took getting the acquisition under control.

Affiliate guilds have gaps as low as three percent and as high as ten. The Bounty Hunters Guild uses a sliding scale, taking small cuts of the cheap, pin-money bounties (so you have enough left over to earn a living wage) and larger cuts of the mid-level ones. For Galactic and Most Wanted bounties, the Guild again takes a smaller gap, as an incentive for the best hunters to tackle the biggest challenges.

You want to keep every cred you collect? Go it alone and see how well you do. The Guild is the best because of what it provides, and like everything else worth having in this galaxy, that's all built on money. And unlike anybody else you're likely to meet—take the so-called Jedi who used to live it up in a trillion-credit Coruscant temple—we're the only ones who are honest about it.

That's not the end of the codes, not by a long shot. Every Guild hunter needs to submit to an evaluation by the Guildmaster's agents at least every three years, or once a year for probationary members. Worried about passing? You probably don't have anything to worry about. That shows you care about your job.

Hunters who let things slip are the ones who should watch their backs. The ones who don't keep their gear running or their permits current. The ones who keep racking up complaints from local law offices—or worse, from clients. Fail an evaluation and you might get a warning, if the Guildmaster's having a good day. Fail two and you're out. No matter what.

GUILD RULES

Following the Bounty Hunters' Creed is the responsibility of *all* hunters, so the additional rules of the Guild go further to clarify the behaviors that make us unique. Obey these, and obey the Creed, and you shouldn't have any trouble with your probationary Guildmaster's evaluation.

1. **Accept the job your Guild contractor gives you.** Guild hunters don't pick whatever hunt sounds like fun. At least, the rookies don't. There's a good reason why you've been kept busy

collaring tax evaders in the Muunilinst banking dens, and your contractor knows it better than you ever will. If you're itching for a fight, handle the easy runs first. You'll get your chance.

2. **Don't question your Guild contractor.** In other words, keep your mouth shut and do your job. I'll question anyone I want! - Bossk

3. **Never deny aid to a Guildmember.** This goes deeper than the Bounty Hunters' Creed, and the reason should be obvious. If the Creed demands that you even help out scrub hunters, how much more should you give to your brothers and sisters in the Bounty Hunters Guild? You give them your right arm, that's how much.

Any Guildmember except Bossk. – Greedo

You're lucky you're already dead. - Bossk

4. **Don't poach in another hunter's territory.** Every time you get a job, your Guild contractor will let you know the planet,

Disputes happen. Let the Guild sort them out.

system, or sector where that job is supposed to go down. If your target scurries, check back with your contractor before chasing the target all the way down the Corellian Run. Different hunters are scoped to work different beats, and that's all you need to know about that.

It goes fists, teeth, and then blasters. - Bossk

5. **Submit any disputes between hunters to the Guild for arbitration.** If it's something you can solve with punches, go right ahead. But if it's the kind of thing where one of you is likely to pull a blaster, *submit it for arbitration*. If you kill or maim the other guy, you just cost the Guild a dues-paying hunter. And guess who's going to repay the lost credits? Call it in and make your accusation. A conclave will be convened within 30 days. These meetings are called hunters' lodges.

TRIAL AND SENTENCING

We keep our own justice. Under Point 5 of the Guild rules above, a hunters' lodge decides the fate of an accused Guildmember. In a sector Guildhouse, a hunters' lodge is held in the combat arena. All available members gather in the stands, and the accused and the accuser face off on the arena floor.

RISKY. TOO MANY HUNTERS IN ONE LOCATION ARE EASY TO AMBUSH. BOBA

Of course, a hunters' lodge can be called just about anywhere, from a starship's hold to a tavern's storage room. You need a minimum of six hunters to listen to the lodgment of accusation. Each party has the right to air their case, and the verdict is determined by a majority vote by the assembled hunters.

A hunter found guilty of violating the Creed has dishonored the bounty hunting profession. The guilty are expelled from the Guild and forever banned from hunting. Even if they try to scratch out a living as independents, they're no longer protected by the Creed's tenets, including "No Hunter Shall Slay Another Hunter." Nobody will get teary-eyed if these types should meet with a bad end.

But most lodge trials boil down to personal grudges, and the related penalties aren't nearly so severe. A hunter who's been judged to be in the wrong might be ordered to fork over a stack of credits, or maybe to settle it with the other hunter in one-on-one combat right there at the lodge. If that happens there are usually no weapons, but then again some Guildhouses love to stage cutlass duels. If you're the kind of mudlicker who's always angering his friends, and if you happen to operate out of the Guildhouse on Castell, then you might want to look into signing up for swordfighting lessons.

The verdict of a hunters' lodge is absolute.

THE BOUNTY

Stripped to its essence, a bounty is a cash incentive for solving cases that wouldn't otherwise get solved. Most of the Guild's work comes through the Imperial Office of Criminal Investigation (IOCI) by way of its government postings on the Imperial Enforcement DataCore.

The posting is a legal instrument, technically a Notice of Civil Remandation (NCR). The instant a bounty notice goes up, the target in question is officially an outlaw and is stripped of the rights of an Imperial citizen.

The bigger the crime, the bigger the payout. They don't call it "having a price on your head" for nothing. Earning that price is what makes hunting a career.

BOUNTY POSTINGS

So where do you find bounties? Short answer: *you* don't. As a probationary Guild member, your contractor—your bounty broker —will feed you a steady stream of jobs. But if you stay alive, you'll start climbing the ranks, and soon you'll have more job flexibility.

If you're a full member looking to line up your own hunts, you can check the Imperial Enforcement DataCore for government bounties. The DataCore has limited access nodes, but those sites include IOCI offices, independent posting agencies, and our own Guildhouses. For all but the last one you'll have to pay up if you want to tap in.

he DataCore too expensive. ny local gency is tter anyway. Greedo

What you see in the DataCore listings depends on where you're at. Most planetary or system bounties are only posted inside their local jurisdictions, which cuts down on clutter and saves money for the one who posted the bounty in the first place.

If you're in the field you're probably not near a Guildhouse, so IOCI offices and posting agencies are going to be your second home. Both of them offer DataCore access and can generate official permits. IOCI offices will even accept delivery of captured acquisitions if they've got holding cells. But Imperial data-pushers at the IOCI have their own business to worry about, so don't be surprised when you get a chilly reception.

You'll probably prefer the posting agencies. Even though they're independently owned they offer most of the same services as the IOCI. Just remember that because they're not government, they need to cover their overhead, and they're going to charge you extra. Posting agencies have set up shop in every starport from Mos Eisley to the Wheel, each of them registered to some local entrepreneur with a not-so-secret underworld connection.

Mos Eisley! They're talk about me! — Greedo

Greedo was as delusional as Bossk. — Dengar

And that's a good thing. Some of the franchised posting agencies, like Rozatta's on Primeday or the Bountiful Mark Emporium, know a whole lot more about the bounties than what's listed on the NCR. If you know the right passphrase, some of these shops will even unlock their cellar arsenals and let you go shopping.

UPDATED LIST: CLASS 4 ARSENALS OR ABOVE
- MOS ESPA, TATOOINE
- BAGSHO, NIW DROUIS
- SKIP 72, SMUGGLER RUN
BOBA

Don't spend too much time hanging around posting agencies, though. Imperial governors might stage a big arrest if a Moff drops by for an inspection and you don't want to risk getting rounded up too. Bounty targets on the Most Wanted list don't like the posting agencies either, because they act as vectors for putting fresh hunters on their trail. There's a story that Dr. Nuvo Vindi gassed every agency on Ord Marsax the day after the Republic upped the bounty on his head to 250,000 credits.

Dr. Vindi led dozens of hunters on a merry chase.

NON-GOVERNMENT BOUNTIES

There are plenty of hunts that don't go through the Imperial Office of Criminal Investigation. In fact, bounty hunters privately contracted by the Hutts or the megacorporations might go their entire careers without ever working an official government hunt.

Underworld bounties are regularly posted on shadowfeeds like Cynabar's Infonet, and any posting agency can tap these hidden nodes if you pay off the right infochant. You can also find some of these bounties in a holofeed scrolling across the wall of a bounty hunter cantina, and if you're carrying a Hunter Imagecaster you can just pass it in front of the display to transfer the data to your own device. This also logs your intention to pursue that bounty.

I need to get one of those Imagecasters. – Greedo

The wine cellar of Fossfog's on Axxila is plugged into every underworld feed.

CURIOUS THAT CRADOSSK ALLOWED THIS TO MAKE IT INTO A RECRUITMENT GUIDE. EVERY HUNTER AT THE BLACKLIST LEVEL LONG AGO LEFT THE GUILD BEHIND.
BOBA

The **Blacklist** is the underworld equivalent of the Most Wanted rankings, but it's only available to the very best hunters in the galaxy. Only certain high-level clients can post to it, so a Blacklist hunt might come from the likes of Baron Tagge, Prince Xizor, or maybe even Lord Vader himself. Besides knowing that the list is out there somewhere, you won't need to take any action when it comes to the Blacklist. If you're good enough someday, the Blacklist will come to you.

Corporate bounties are backed up by billion-credit operating budgets. You can stuff your pockets if you're willing to grit your teeth through business headaches like filing every bounty claim in triplicate. Corporate bounties are just as legitimate as IOCI bounties and are sometimes listed in the governmental DataCore, a holdover from when the Trade Federation, the InterGalactic Banking Clan, and the Commerce Guild held more power than the entire Republic Senate.

Those days aren't entirely gone, if TaggeCo and Sienar Fleet Systems are anything to go by. And if you're hoping to do jobs in the Corporate Sector, corporate bounties are the only game in town. No matter what's listed on the bounty posting, companies will almost always pay you more when you reach out to them directly. Contact the Human Resources department, Crimson Trade division.

There are also **private bounties**, which any citizen can post so long as they put up the money in advance and provide some documentation of the alleged crime. These bounties often happen when lovers' quarrels go sour, and the payout usually stinks. Leave them for independent hunters to gnaw on.

The last big provider of bounties—and also the newest—is the **Imperial Security Bureau**. The ISB's listings aren't traditional government bounties, because nobody on the lists has committed what you'd consider a crime. And that right there, believe it or not, is the sunny side of living under the Empire. *More hunts for hunters.*

Sunny side. That's a good one.

— Dengar

The ISB's Enforcement Division effectively tripled the number of enforceable offenses when it added things like "failure to comply with the precepts of Emperor Palpatine's New Order." What does that even mean? Absolutely anything the ISB wants it to.

The ISB's bounty postings are known as LAACDocs, for Legal Authorization for Advanced Containment. And its list of suspects is as long as a Gungan's tongue. Technically, because there's no crime, there's no bounty, but that just means the ISB calls it an "honorarium" and it's business as usual.

Acquisitions you bring in under LAACDocs are detained indefinitely by the ISB on the authority of Emperor Palpatine's High Inquisitors. You can bet you'll never see those poor barves again.

But maybe you have a problem rounding up rebels? Not too many hunters like it. It's not my favorite job either, but these are the times we live in. And have you seen how much the ISB'll pay for Princess Leia Organa? If you've got the skills, you can start dreaming of that regatta yacht on Spira again.

Let her come to Tatooine. I'll get her. – Greedo

BOUNTY CLASSIFICATIONS

Bigger crimes equal bigger payouts. Except for all the times when a client throws a fortune on the head of somebody who humiliated them over something small. It happens all the time, and all in the name of pride.

But in general there's a predictable incentive riser baked into the system. From biggest to smallest, here's how the IOCI and the Bounty Hunters Guild classify hunts:

MOST WANTED
(BOUNTY RANGE: IN EXCESS OF 200,000 CREDITS)

These are the big dragfish, the ones the Empire calls imminent threats to public safety or Imperial security. The money is great, but don't be stupid enough to think of these as your retirement tickets. Everybody on the Most Wanted list is there for a reason, one that could be purely political

I'd like to see Boba on the list.
- Bossk

but could also involve some serious mayhem. At the very least, a criminal on this list has done an incredible job of avoiding capture. That's why they're now our problem, and not buried in some law officer's case file.

Killers and maniacs on the Most Wanted list are usually marked "dead or alive." Political dissidents are marked "locate and detain," which means *don't shoot* unless you're sure the target is going to survive a blaster bolt where you're aiming.

You took out a walker? Welcome to the Most Wanted list.

Crimes that land people on the Most Wanted list include:

- Conspiracy, sedition, or treason against the Empire.
- Destruction/theft of Imperial property valued in excess of 250,000 credits.
- Impersonation of an Imperial official.
- Flight to avoid Imperial prosecution.
- Obstruction of Imperial authority.

That last one is vague on purpose and is often used to justify some petty power trips. Lots of people will complain to your face about it, but like I always tell them, we bounty hunters are just the messengers. If they want to get mad at someone, they can go shake their fists at a Grand Moff.

GALACTIC

(BOUNTY RANGE: 50,000–200,000 CREDITS)

These sleemos aren't bad enough to land on the Most Wanted list, but they've earned a galaxy-wide bounty just the same. The Galactic list is tens of thousands of names long (where the Most Wanted list is only a few hundred), and some of them have been listed for decades. Don't expect any hunts at this level from your Guild contractor. By the time you're ready to tackle a Galactic bounty, you'll have long since earned the right to pick your own hunts. I was born to tackle these high-level bounties. – Greedo

Zero-gee boarding of a drone barge. This makes the Empire angry.

Crimes for landing on the Galactic list include:

- Aggression against a member of the Imperial armed forces.
- Bribery of an Imperial official. I can name 17 systems where it's a crime NOT to bribe Imps. – Dengar
- Transportation of restricted items. This is a bigger offense than simple smuggling, and usually means stolen prototypes or superweapon plans.
- Piracy. Especially those Rim-runners who prey on Imperial drone barges.
- Possession of a cloaking device. After the stygium mines ran

dry, cloaking tech became the Empire's little secret. What you should know about this particular crime is that the Imperials don't care as much about the person as they do about the person's ship.

REGIONAL
(BOUNTY RANGE: 20,000–75,000 CREDITS)

Like it says, a regional bounty is offered only within a specific galactic region, the Core Worlds excepted. That can be anything from Colonies, Inner Rim, Expansion Region, Mid Rim, and Outer Rim all the way to specialty haunts like the Centrality. Notable exceptions are the Corporate Sector and Hutt Space, where local officials direct their own bounty operations independently of the IOCI.

Eight out of every ten regional bounties are posted within the Outer Rim Territories, so get used to it. It's the biggest place for a target to hide.

Beneath its hull this tanker is probably stuffed with illegal modifications.

Crimes that will earn somebody a spot on the regional bounty list include:

- Murder of Imperial government personnel. Regular old murder isn't enough to rate a regional bounty.

I wonder if the
-mpire knows about
Solo's ship. I'd love
o see him burn.
– Greedo

- Forgery. A good forger can reproduce anything from an IPKC to a 100,000 credit note, and a good forger is smart enough to not get caught. A forger who's earned a Regional bounty probably got backstabbed by a partner (which, if you're smart, is where you should start your hunt).
- Operating an unlawful starship. A private freighter that's got military-grade shielding and a torpedo rack is breaking dozens of laws just by existing. It's rare to see a bounty posted for this crime, but it can happen if a captain skips out on the Bureau of Ships and Services' annual shakedown.
- Transporting stolen goods. This one is on the books to target the smuggling kingpins who regularly move million-credit payloads. When you track one of them down, don't be surprised when they offer double or triple the bounty value to buy you off. I trust you know by now that nothing comes between a hunter and an acquisition.

SECTOR, SYSTEM, AND PLANETARY (BOUNTY RANGE: 3,000–50,000 CREDITS)

These bounties are offered within a specific sector, system, or planet's gravity well. They'll probably only show up when you're searching a localized node of the DataCore. Even though they don't have big payouts, a decent hunter can collar this level of low-grade merchandise again and again, making more in pin money than they would if they spent half a year tracking Jaarl the Conqueror to score a single big payday.

Here's what lands somebody on this list:

- Aiding and abetting criminal activity.
- Murder.
- Kidnapping.
- Transportation of passengers in violation of customs laws.
- Possession of an illegal weapon.
- Smuggling. These are usually small jobs.

I'll bet Solo's ship is totally illegal.
— Greedo

I had no idea Greedo was so pre-occupied with me.
— Han Solo

- Operating an illegally modified starship. Usually the equipment is legal, but somebody forgot to get the permits.
- Breaking into an Imperial installation.
- Jamming official communications.

CORPORATE BOUNTIES

That's it for IOCI bounties, but the rules are different when somebody other than the government puts a price on a head. Corporate bounties, for example, have almost nothing to do with public safety. What kinds of crimes will make an exec mad enough to hire a hunter? It's all about protecting their profit statements:

- Industrial espionage.
- Theft or destruction of corporate property.
- Criminal trespass on company facilities.
- Unauthorized use of company databases.
- Malicious corruption of company records.
- Attempted bribery or intimidation of company employees.
- Illegal replication of a trademarked device.
- Violation of a company's security agreement.

Corporations aren't too happy when somebody steals their trade secrets.

UNDERWORLD BOUNTIES

Underworld bounties, by contrast, are always a surprise. You'll see lots of death marks slapped on the heads of majordomos who stole from their masters or who turned traitor by testifying for Imperial prosecutors. But because a good chunk of these bounties are posted by the clan leaders on Nal Hutta, a "crime" can be anything that made a Hutt cranky. A chef who put too many fleek eels in the pudding, for example. An animal wrangler for the dungeon menagerie who was on duty when the nos monster died of old age.

I remember one singer, 20,000 on his head, and all he did was mispronounce the Huttese *grantu chato* ("wondrous one") as *grantu choto* ("wondrous runt"). Sure I felt bad when I turned him over to Ziro's goons, and I sighed a little when I saw them toss him out the window of Ziro's 700th-floor penthouse. But a smart hunter goes where the credits are.

Ziro had no sense of humor, but he paid well.

HUNTING PERMITS

Bounty hunters aren't vigilantes. So while you might not like all the data-work, you still have to file it. There's no point in complaining about this, and besides, Guild contractors will take most of the tedium out of your hands. Government regulations are a side effect of working legitimate.

As a probationary member of the Bounty Hunters Guild, you can count on your Guild bounty broker to line up hunts based on your skill level, the necessary gear, the number of competing independent hunters already working the case, the cost of starship fuel to travel from one jurisdiction to the next, and the types of required permits. There are a lot of permits.

Does Boba Fett carry an IPKC? - Greedo

Every bounty hunter needs to carry a current Imperial Peacekeeping Certificate (IPKC). It's 500 credits, payable to the Imperial Office of Criminal Investigation (IOCI), and is subject to annual renewal. The IPKC replaced the Republic Certificate of Deputization about twenty years back as a hunter's license to operate. Specifically, it lays down these rules of engagement under Imperial law:

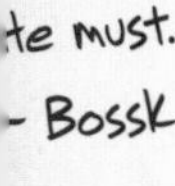

I doubt it. - Dengar

1. The bounty poster reserves the right to determine proper treatment of the acquisition.

2. Injury, incapacitation, or death of an acquisition may only occur if the subject has refused to surrender.

3. Only a clear and reasonable application of force may be used against an acquisition.

4. A licensed bounty hunter will not accept any illegal, private, or informal contract that is not legally recognized within the Empire.

That last point isn't surprising. It's an Imperial government document, don't forget. So I'll just note that not all bounty hunters read that far down and leave it at that.

Keep your cool going through starport customs.

Your IPKC also gives you a law-enforcement waiver on weapons restrictions. You can carry that blaster rifle through starport customs no problem, but the more exotic stuff, like biocorruptors and heavy explosives, can still land you in a pot of trouble.

Besides the IPKC, each hunt might require an armful of specialty permits:

- A **Target Permit** gives you the right of extradition to transport a capture across sector and regional borders. Target permits are unique to bounties, meaning you have to get one for each acquisition you're actively pursuing. The cost is 100–1,000 credits per month.

When I get my own starship, I'll get my sector permit. – Greedo

- A **Sector Permit** authorizes you to operate within the bounds of a designated sector in pursuit of a bounty for that sector. But doesn't the IPKC already cover this? You'd think so, but then you'd be forgetting how strong bureaucrats squeeze when they're wringing out that last drop of money. Sector permits are required for mid-level bounties (with payouts of 10,000 credits or more) and cost 1,000–10,000 credits per month to keep active.

- A **System Permit** authorizes you to operate among the planets, moons, and space stations of a particular star system. So do you have to get a system permit even if you already have a sector permit that covers the same territory? You'd better believe it. System permits run between 50 and 500 credits per month.

- In case you didn't have time to get all your datawork in order before a successful takedown, a **Capture Permit** gives you retroactive authorization for all of the above. Capture permits can save your hide, but don't use them as safety nets for a lack of preparation. The IOCI gouges you on capture permits for exactly that reason. In some jurisdictions it's as much as 25 percent of the total bounty, and that's coming out of your piece of the payout. Not the Guild's.

Some regions of the galaxy, including the Core Worlds and the Hapes Consortium, are officially No Hunt Zones. But that just means you need to slip a bribe to the right official and operate discreetly. Some call this "filing the gray permit." If you're heading to Byblos or some other port where everybody's on the take, the Guild might even float you a credit line just for bribes.

The mug who wrote this can't decide whether bribing Imps is forbidden or necessary. — Dengar

Some hunters try to cut the bureaucrats out of the picture by running sectors. They'll pretend to just be passing through, then secretly transport their bounty capture into a no-permit sector before claiming the payout. Expect jail time if you're caught—and it's against Guild policy, so don't expect your bounty broker to bail you out.

PURSUING MULTIPLE BOUNTIES

There's nothing to prevent more than one client from putting a bounty on the head of a single unlucky barve. And there's nothing to stop you from cashing in on it.

Dostryt's been milking this
Glottalphib story for years.
— Dengar

Look at an example. Say there's a pyromaniac on the loose. A Glottalphib who lost his voice, maybe, and now uses a flame-sprayer to spit fire. So this sleemo is wanted for arson by the owner of a featherbed factory on Hijo. He gets away, but earns another price on his head when he sneaks a CZ-28 Flamestrike through Ichalin Station customs. Then he decides to lay low, but accidentally flicks ash on the sleeve of the Imperial governor of Bilbringi, who's so outraged he puts out a warrant on the firebug for "sedition against the Empire." It's a bad day for the Glottalphib, but a good day for you if you can work the angles and collect three bounties for the price of one boxhead. And that's why we have Guild contractors.

I'm skipping over the capture part, but let's say you've got him restrained in your ship's hold. Your first choice is where to turn him in and claim your bounty. Most hunters will go straight for the biggest listed payout, but a contractor who's sniffed around will know which clients might pay a *secondary* bounty with proof of capture. Handing the Glottalphib over

Made a capture? Congratulations. Now maximize your profits.

to that factory owner might net you a lower payout of 50,000 credits (where the governor was promising 60,000), but the governor might have such a nerf up his nose about the whole thing that he'll pay you 25,000—a bargain, from his perspective, just for the pleasure of watching a holo of a jail cell sealing shut on the miserable fireslug.

METHODS OF PAYMENT

Once you turn your captured merchandise over to a receiver, it's time to collect what you're owed. If it's a bounty that's been prepaid to the Imperial Office of Criminal Investigation you can get your credits directly from an IOCI office accountant. Regular clients of the Bounty Hunters Guild usually make direct transfers into Guild accounts. Just show the receipt to a Guild numbercruncher and you'll get your cut.

If you need to collect payment from a client yourself, demand the money on a slicer-proof credit stick or in the form of a verified Imperial Warrant. The latter will let you withdraw the amount in credit notes from any Imperial bank.

There are lots of other ways to get paid, and when you work the Outer Rim you'll see them all. Don't laugh in the face of a shaak rancher who wants to pay you with livestock—at least not until after you've checked on the market price of shaak meat. Some of these methods might benefit the Guild in the long run, and all have been accepted as hunt compensation in the past:

- **Rights of Salvage.** This usually means you get to keep whatever belonged to the acquisition, including starships, and storage lockers—and all the stuff that's inside. It's a gamble, but the odds improve when your target is a weapons engineer or a hoarder of rare artworks.

MISSING TOO MANY SECRET COMPARTMENTS. NEED TO ACQUIRE:
- MOLECULAR SCANNER
- TRAP SPRINGERS
- COLD-BURNING FUSIONCUTTER (CHECK WITH ROZATTA)

BOBA

- **Land Grants, Mining Permits, and Water Rights.** These are lifeblood resources on the frontier, so cash-poor outland planets sometimes extend them to pay off their debts. Try getting credits on the blaster head first, but resource rights can turn into long-term money streams if the colony sticks around long enough to grow into a settlement.

- **Corporate Stock.** Don't be stupid and accept this without checking with your Guild contractor. Don't go by how comfy you thought the couches were in the corporate office. A piece of a failing company is worthless, but a piece of a winner could be huge. The Bounty Hunters Guild holds stock in some of the galaxy's cornerstone corporations. If Guildmaster Cradossk demanded a sit-down with the heads of Lerrimore or Ayelixe/Krongbing, they'd trip over their desks to greet him.

Why would my fool father even want to meet with droid and textile manufacturers
- Bossk

Lerrimore Droids provides discounts on KPR servant droids to all Guild members.

- **Precious Goods.** Most of these items have a set market value, and you should be able to negotiate the quantity based on that. Common goods offered as currency on Rim worlds include:

    Spice. From the least valuable to the most valuable, the main varieties are andris, ryll, booster blue, carsunum, lesai, glitterstim, and lumni-spice.

    Nova crystals or other gems regularly traded as currency like fire nodes or glow-pearls.

Precious metals like aurodium.

Megonite moss. This one is *highly volatile*. Transport it in stasis lockers only.

Rare jewelry, including Eriaduan shellwork or anything made by the Meshakians.

Woven bolts of toumon or veda cloth.

Raw or refined tibanna gas.

Unless you have a refrigerated cargo hold (or a very, very fast ship), never accept payment in perishable luxury foods like rikknit eggs. You'll land at your next stop carrying nothing of value, and you'll never be able to get the rot-stink out of your upholstery.

And don't worry about getting stiffed. Bounty hunting is a business, and nobody in a position of authority will risk their status by ignoring a legal debt outright. If they do, remember that you're running with the Bounty Hunters Guild. Nobody, not even the Zanibar cannibals of Xo, wants to get on the Guild's bad side.

Zanibar meat is delicious.
- Bossk

CONTRACTOR RESOURCES

The Guild didn't get where it is by leaving money on the table. The Guild's contractors are smarter than you are, and they probably earn more credits too. Listen to what they tell you. They don't want your hunt to go bad any more than you do.

So where do the contractors obtain their info? There are millions of informants and shadownet feeds out there, but the Guild's weirdest asset by far is the Ghostling Nest of the Assembler. It's drifting somewhere out beyond Wild Space, in case you heard it was a spacer legend.

The nest is big enough to park a starship inside and it looks like a ginntho spider's funnel web, but its pale gray strands are actually living neural cords. Half-buried in its tangled heart is the Assembler, who spins neurofibers linking the little bugs that crawl the walls to act as eyes and ears.

The Ghostling Nest, or at least a recent configuration of it

As you approach the nest from the outside, you'll see the silver glint of turbolasers and missile tubes—just in case you had any ideas about squashing this particular insect hive.

The Assembler's home is also its brain. Somehow its info is always fresh, and the bug itself is so smart it'll give you the shivers. The Bounty Hunters Guild has worked with the Assembler and its predecessors for generations, and the Ghostling Nest is considered neutral ground for the receipt and transfer of bounty payments and the temporary custody of bounty captures. The Assembler acts as a trustworthy intermediary, which has convinced many skeptics to do business with the Guild since the buffer of the Ghostling Nest lets them claim ignorance if a hunt goes spectacularly bad.

You won't visit the Ghostling Nest as a rookie. Its coordinates are unknown to everybody except our master hunters. But you'll hear plenty of creepy tales if you hang around the Guild hall, and pretty soon you'll stop squashing bugs and start politely shooing them away instead. Me, I

~~LAST LOCATION: COORDINATES -334, -698, 19, OUTER RIM, MODDELL SECTOR~~ BOBA

UPDATE: MOVED TO COORDINATES -299, -701, -20, WILD SPACE NEAR HOAG'S DECANT think the Assembler's secret is that it has its little bug-spies *everywhere*. Who knows if that lurking beetle is actually an eye cluster beaming everything back to the Ghostling Nest?

The Guild has other secrets, too, and some of its proprietary resources are kept tightly under wraps. In the Guild's data vault on Fusai there's supposedly a holotracer that can track any HoloNet transmission back to its source. I didn't believe it at first, because encrypted comm transmissions that come from military, government, and underworld sources are masked with S-thread dupes and message noise. But they say a blackmailed Gree built the holotracer for the Japrael sector Separatists back during the Clone Wars, and that the Guild got it from Legate Lux Bonteri before the war's end. I've never seen the device myself, but it's possible the Guild's contractors have used it to gather info on every one of my hunts over the last 20 years. I've got no way of knowing for sure, but I'm glad the contractors are on our side.

Is this guy writing a handbook or a gossip column?
– Dengar

The Assembler sometimes calls itself Kud'ar Mub'at.

OUR HISTORY

Weeyo?
Not this old blowhard.
- Bossk

BY KENEK WEEYO,

CHIEF CUSTODIAN OF THE BOUNTY HUNTERS GUILD

MUSEUM AND LIBRARY

I've been in charge of the Guild Museum and Library for a long time, and, over the years, more than a few young bounty hunters have told me that they had little interest in history, that they were more interested in the present and in moments yet to come. They behaved like muscle for hire, but I suppose that's all they were. I'm sorry to say each was killed while pursuing a bounty, long before reaching middle age, let alone a comfortable retirement.

But take heart! They died needlessly only if you follow their example. Our line of work can take you all over the galaxy, and if you set foot on any world without knowing poodoo about how your predecessors hunted and survived, you might as well hang a "blast me" sign around your neck. If you don't want to know about the past, you'll never learn and, most likely, won't survive.

I'm not writing this for my amusement. Skip it if you must, and, with regret, I will add your name to the lamentably long list of dunderheads who refused to understand.

Still with me? Congratulations. Our recruits get smarter all the time.

THE BIRTH OF THE GUILD

Since long before the founding of the Galactic Republic, countless bounty hunters have prowled the galaxy, tracking acquisitions. Although many hunters operated alone, many also formed alliances. Whether these hunters teamed up to tackle a single bounty or to cooperate with other law-enforcement agencies within specific areas of space on an ongoing basis, they knew the advantage of strength in numbers and dependable reinforcements.

Historic records indicate various incarnations of the Bounty Hunters Guild over the past 25,000 years. The earliest records date to shortly after the formation of the Galactic Republic, with a guild in the Kashyyyk system. This guild was essentially a social club for Trandoshan hunters and their sons, but Trandoshans take great pride in the fact that their Guild was the first. Over the course of centuries, hunters from other systems formed guilds, and some of these guilds—including the Trandoshans'—became affiliated as the Bounty Hunters Guild. Although this guild operated more like a coalition of associations than a unified professional organization, historical accounts describe this group of hunters as a notably efficient group.

It should have stay that way. - Bossk

When not hunting and killing, Trandoshans enjoy listening to tales of hunting and killing.

Guild members occasionally worked alongside Jedi. These partnerships included numerous hunts during the Great Hyperspace War. Some remote civilizations developed the mistaken idea that bounty hunters *served* the Jedi, a false perspective that the Guild must still correct from time to time. The Guild did not encounter any significant competition until it began losing Neimoidian contracts to Gank mercenaries. Although this situation created greater solidarity among the more disciplined members of the Bounty Hunters Guild, some younger Guild members took inspiration from the Gank mercenaries and began secretly selling their skills to the highest bidder. Eventually, many Guild members were openly advertising themselves as soldiers for hire, and an alarming number gave no thought to matters of honor or dignity. By the time of the Mandalorian Wars, the Guild's organization was so fractured and compromised by mercenary activity that the Guild's leader, the Trandoshan Vossk, quit in disgust.

While the Guild was still splintered by mercenary factions, an independent human bounty hunter named Calo Nord came into prominence during the Jedi Civil War. By all accounts, Nord appeared harmless, but he was in fact deadly. Sold into slavery by his own parents, he was only a young man of sixteen when he killed his slavers, then tracked his parents down and killed them, too. A bounty was placed on his head, and Nord killed every hunter who came after him. He became a bounty hunter himself, and, in a matter of years, his name was the most feared in the Outer Rim. No one ever disputed the widely held belief that he silenced more people than the Iridian Plague. Rumor had it that Nord was killed on Tatooine, but his legacy cast a wide shadow over the profession of bounty hunting. Centuries later, the Guild continues to have a difficult time convincing civilians that not all hunters are Calo Nord.

After the Battle of Ruusan, which left scores of Jedi Knights and their Force-using Sith Lord enemies dead, there occurred several notorious conflicts between undercover Jedi and bounty hunters in the Colonies and Inner Rim. Unfortunately, all the conflicts took place while the Jedi and the bounty hunters were unwittingly pursuing the same criminals. Subsequently, the Galactic Senate proposed that bounty hunters should follow the example of the Jedi Order, and create a governing body to organize themselves and communicate more openly with other law-enforcement agencies.

Many independent hunters scoffed at the idea of organizing under a ruling body, but four influential clan leaders were quick to recognize the practical aspects of some kind of union. These leaders were Thrassk of Trandosha, Teesoo of Rodia, the Twi'lek outcast Saya Ksi, and Keekrim Pon of Corellia. Banding together, they wrote the Bounty Hunters' Creed, and founded what was then called the New Bounty Hunters Guild. According to their vision, the Guild would unite hunters under specific rules and regulations, promote the training of apprentices in the ways of hunting, and encourage hunters to collaborate with one another. To appease the Senate, the Creed's authors also outlined how the Guild and Jedi Order could work together to meet their goals.

Guild founders Thrassk, Teesoo, Saya Ksi, and Keekrim Pon

Many independent hunters were skeptical of the Guild's chances of success, but their attitude changed when they realized Guild members received advance notice on the Republic's highest-paying bounties. As for the Guild working with the Jedi, joint missions were problematic almost from the start, no doubt because the Jedi regarded bounty hunters as obstacles to their goal of conquering the Republic.

Almost 900 years ago, a schism occurred within the Guild, when a faction of human Guild hunters formed a humans-only confederacy. All the members of this faction were killed in a massive explosion that destroyed the space station at Ixtlar, where they'd attempted to hold their first meeting. The cause of the explosion was never determined, but persistent rumors implied that a group of Guild hunters, one that included humans, was responsible for killing the defectors. After the deaths at Ixtlar, the Guild began a vigorous campaign to recruit hunters of many different species from across the galaxy, and they promoted the Guild as a truly egalitarian organization, which it remains to this day. Even droids are allowed to join the Guild.

RUMORS WERE WRONG. THE MANDALORIANS DID THAT JOB TO RETALIATE FOR HUMAN GUILD HUNTERS INVADING THEIR TERRITORY. BOBA

The Ixtlar incident saved the Guild.

So as you travel throughout the galaxy in service of the Bounty Hunters Guild, know that you are part of a long history of hunters. Remember that the Guild Museum and Library holds thousands of biographies and instructional datatapes. The more you learn about your predecessors and their experiences, the better chance you'll have to survive misfortune, make a profit, and keep the Guild going strong for generations to come.

AN ANCIENT PROFESSION

The profession of hunting criminals for profit has been around for thousands of years. If there's an official record that pinpoints where and when it had its origin, I've never seen it. But it's an easy guess that bounty hunting began on the first planet that had all the right things going for it: a dangerous criminal element, an overwhelmed or nonexistent law-enforcement organization, weapons, and some kind of monetary system.

One of the earliest historic accounts of an interplanetary bounty hunter is preserved by way of ancient glyphs etched upon a metal wall on the planet Thokos. The glyphs date back approximately twenty-five millennia. The following text is the traditional translation of the glyphs:

I've seen the glyphs. They're fascinating. – Dengar

> "A long time ago, a bloodthirsty gangster seized power in the Thokos system. Many lawmen and civilians died trying to kill or escape from the fiend, and it seemed all hope was lost. A group of villagers on Thokos transmitted a plea to other worlds, and promised a reward of precious crystals to anyone who could help. Many months passed before a one-eyed stranger carrying a long, glowing spear arrived by starship. She faced the villagers and said, "I will dispose of your oppressor. But first, you will show me the crystals so I can see they are authentic."
>
> "How can we know you will help us? How can we know you won't kill us and steal the crystals?"
>
> "I am a hunter, not a liar, assassin, or thief. Our word is our contract, and I always honor a contract."
>
> The village leaders brought forth the crystals. The hunter examined the crystals, found them satisfactory, and departed for the gangster's lair.
>
> Three days later, as night was falling, the hunter returned, clutching her spear in one hand and the gangster's head in another. The hunter was limping, and she used her spear as a walk-

The suitably bloody legend of Thokos

ing stick to guide her progress. A wide bandage covered her one eye. “My prey blinded me,” she said, “but my job is done. You will give me the crystals, and I ask one of you to guide me back to my starship.”

But the leader of the village saw an opportunity to deceive the hunter. He gave her a bag filled with small, worthless stones instead of the promised crystals. Scheming to take her ship as well, he said his people could not guide her to her ship until daylight, but he invited her to join them in celebrating the gangster’s death. As the celebration proceeded, the villagers did not notice the hunter limp away into the surrounding darkness, taking the bag of stones with her.

Later that night, the village leader collapsed upon the ground. The other villagers bent over his unconscious body and discovered he had been stunned by a single small stone. And then they heard the hunter’s voice from the shadows.

“Your leader attempted to cheat me of the crystals that I earned. My injuries and loss of vision have not affected my aim. I have many stones, enough for each of you. Bring me the crystals, or when your leader awakens, he will find all of you dead.”

The villagers looked at each other and trembled. One cried out, “What kind of monster are you?”

The hunter sighed before she answered, “Not the kind who would break a contract.”

And to you, novice, I say the same. Be a monster if you must, but be the right kind of monster. The honorable kind. The kind the Guild can be proud to claim.

MY FATHER TOLD ME A DIFFERENT VERSION OF THIS STOR
THE VILLAGERS ATTACKED THE HUNTER, AND THE HUNTER KILLE
THEM ALL IN
SELF-DEFEN
BOBA

THE HUNT

BY RO-SAN BOROKKI,

DIRECTOR OF TRAINING, 18-YEAR VETERAN OF THE GUILD

You have to clear a few hunts just to qualify for membership in the Bounty Hunters Guild. But once you qualify, you still don't know *how* to hunt, not on the Guild's level. It's your responsibility to get there, and fast.

SEPI

Centuries of pooled experience by Guildmembers led to the SEPI principle, which is still the best distillation of what goes into a successful hunt. It's a simple but endlessly adaptable framework. Under SEPI, every hunt consists of four consecutive stages: Selection, Evaluation, Preparation, and Implementation.

PHASE 1: SELECTION

Most hunts that go bad were bad from the beginning. It happened when the wrong hunter chose the wrong target.

Does a mark have a huge price on his head, or a bounty that's gone unclaimed for years? It makes a big difference whether he's deadly or just slippery, and whether you have the skills to match. You might be a good tracker, but are you the right kind of tracker? Are you a jungle scout when what's really needed is a data slicer?

Matching hunters with hunts is a Guild specialty, and getting Phase 1 right is a big reason why the Guild's success rate is so high. We took a painstaking look at your background when you turned in that application fee, and you didn't even know it.

WENT ROGUE. CURRENT BOUNTY 65,000 CREDITS. LAST SIGHTED AT TEMPLE OF HIS HORNED HIGHNESS ON AGAMAR. BoBA

Somebody in the Guild thinks you have an ability that could come in handy one day, and it's probably not what you think. Sure, a Gamorrean's a good close-up fighter. But a Gamorrean is also the only one who can infiltrate a slushtime sty on a Gamor colony and get within striking distance of an outlaw chieftain, which might be what the Guild really needs.

We've got holy leaders in our ranks, including a High Priest of Dim-U who's a crack shot with a crossbow and who can convince believers to turn *themselves* in. We've got galaxy-class champions in sabacc and pazaak who can play their way inside high-roller casino rooms where debtors like to hole up. It all comes down to trust and how we can exploit it.

If you're not his target, the High Priest might give you a blessing.

Who knows, you might have grown up playing smashball with a kid who will wind up on the Most Wanted list someday. If that happened, you'd be the Guild's best chance.

PHASE 2: EVALUATION

You wouldn't sip a drink without knowing what the bartender poured. So why dive into a hunt without a full understanding of the risks? Independent hunters do a half-job with this step and they wind up dead. Worse, by getting killed they tip off the target that they're being hunted, and that makes our jobs harder. Don't do that.

Take your time during Phase 2 and work with your Guild contractor. A methodical evaluation takes weeks or even months, and should remain open for the duration of the hunt as you uncover new info.

At the start of this phase you'll get a data dump of everything your bounty broker dug up. This will include the target's biography, employment history, ship registrations, and the coordinates of the last known residence. You don't expect somebody with a price on their head to stay put, but you'd be surprised how many make the mistake of begging for help from family members and old friends. Expand your search to the target's network of secondary contacts.

In the last few years the Empire has made it almost impossible to scratch your ear without leaving a data trail behind. The HoloNet is your friend, and you can call in a Guild slicer for help in exchange for a cut of the bounty. This part of Phase 2 is called the skip trace.

A good slicer can tap into comm databases, flagging messages to or from the target and using voice-print matching and predictive language recognition to work around disguises. Bank records are big, and by monitoring a target's accounts you can track credit transfers and bar tabs. What about starports? Your target might be traveling under an alias and a false ship registration, but there probably aren't many YT-1500 freighters out there that have the dorsal docking claw variant—at least not ones captained by a Farghul who's 1.5 meters tall.

Finally, you need to make a threat assessment. Based on everything you've found so far, will the target surrender? Fight to the death? Will their friends give them shelter or sell them out?

There's a reason why most bounties on the Most Wanted list are Rebel Alliance officers. Whatever you think of their politics, the rebels protect their own. They have the firepower to back it up, too. Do you think the Empire hasn't *tried* to capture Mon Mothma or General Carlist Rieekan? It's just that after seeing a couple hundred TIEs get blown up by rebel X-wings, the Empire figured it was easier to offer money than to replace machinery.

othing
pecial
bout
bels. They
ie like
veryone
else.
- Bossk

Mon Mothma. The payout for her capture is astronomical.

If you have any doubts about your hunt after running the threat assessment, stop here before going on to Phase 3. Don't raise your bet if you're holding a losing hand.

PHASE 3: PREPARATION

Time to gear up. What to bring depends on your style of capture. A shadow hunter relies on sabotage, destroying the target's resource caches and terrorizing him into making a mistake. A detection hunter (some of us call them mynocks) will plant tracking devices, then follow the target until he's backed into a corner. One of those hunters needs spy equipment. The other needs thermal detonators.

My blaster is all the preparation I need. – Greedo

Mama and Papa probably told you to be prepared for everything. They were wrong. Recognize that you can't do it all, and make sure you've got the basics covered instead. Stay flexible. Above all, don't get caught short at the one thing you're good at.

Remember, with the right equipment you can make your own luck. (See "Tools of the Trade," p. 73, for more about gearing up.)

A shadow hunter (left) and a detection hunter

PHASE 4: IMPLEMENTATION

Implementation is all about finishing the job you've started. Outsiders think this is all bounty hunters do. Nobody understands that when a hunter spends weeks lining up the first three phases, Phase 4 can be a simple fetch-and-carry job.

But it probably won't be. During the Implementation phase you'll actually hit the field. Hands-on investigation will take the place of the data-work you did in Phase 2. And two methods you'll be using a lot are bribery and intimidation.

Sometimes you won't need either. Burned business partners and heart-broken lovers will tell you every secret you ever wanted to know, asking for nothing in return except the possibility that you'll deal out some damage. Ulic Qel-Droma betrayed his brother during the Great Sith War, and you need to find *your* Ulic. Every family has one.

e Great
ith War?
nat's
cient
story!
Bossk

It's all social engineering, and it'll work best if you're a good listener. People like opening up to somebody they trust. However, if you've got a worrt-ugly face that makes babies cry, you can always fall back on bribery and intimidation.

No matter how you get your subjects talking, you'll want to know if they're lying. Here's what you do: Mention how it's a lovely day we're having, and wouldn't they agree? Or ask them if the saltlicker steak's good at this joint. Or ask them anything else bone-dry boring, which they've got zero reason to lie about. It's called establishing a baseline. You want to see what they look like when they're not working against you.

After you start the interrogation, you look for tells. I'm talking about beads of sweat. Shifty eyes. Twitchy limbs. Trembling voices. A forked tongue that keeps flicking out to taste the air. The spicy smell of fear pheromones. A nictitating membrane that slides in place and clouds the outer eyes. Overexplaining something simple, or filling silences with pointless mouthgas. Skin or scales that flush red as the subject unconsciously prepares a "fight or flight" response. You should also check for microexpressions, which will flash terror or relief for only a fraction of a second and give a window into the subject's true mental state. This kind of stuff is nearly universal among intelligent beings, and paying attention to it doesn't cost you a thing.

Nothing escapes these eyes. – Greedo

Don't look away during an interrogation. You could miss something crucial.

What if you discover they're lying? Slamming a face into a table won't cause permanent damage, but the broken nose or blackened eye will show everybody else you mean business. Just don't try that kind of thing too close to an Imperial garrison. You'll spend a couple days in a holding cell as the trail grows cold.

After you've followed your leads and identified where your target is hidden away, don't rush in. Get the lay of the land first with a treetop stakeout and a pair of macrobinocs. Or slip some credits to the locals to hear their gossip about the target's comings and goings.

Eventually you're going to have to make the shift from observation to neutralization. Do you throw on a disguise and get close to the target as a sanitation scrubber? Maybe trigger a radiation alarm and try to flush the target out into the open? Or do you wait until the dead of night and sneak inside wearing a white-noise stealth suit? Or stride in through the main gate at midday, blasters blazing?

In these pages there's no right answer. Every hunter has their own approach to the takedown. Take Sallow Violect, an ex-Nova Guard still bound by honor. She loudly challenges every target to a public showdown, and somehow she's still breathing. Or Wrencess, a master seducer whose advances have never been rejected by anyone of any species. He spends weeks romancing his targets before revealing his true goal.

The important thing is to know when it's time to strike. Once you're committed, act with intent. Plans can go bad no matter how well you've set everything up, but the Guild can still help you prepare for the worst.

SURVIVING THE HUNT

The Bounty Hunters Guild has invested in your career. It's important to the Guild that you mature into a money generator, and that means keeping you alive until you reach that threshold. Every time you breathe the air of an unfamiliar planet, you're going to run up against something you'd rather you didn't. If you pay attention to these survival pointers you can extend your career by decades.

ESCAPING AN AMBUSH

If you find yourself trading blaster shots with your bounty target, things took a bad turn somewhere. You usually want to deliver your acquisition alive, and you can't do that if he's got a hole in his head. But high-profile targets usually have high-priced backup. If you ask the wrong question in a crowded cantina, you might find yourself staring into a dozen drawn guns while the band dives for cover behind the stage. Finding a defensible position in a firefight is a skill that veteran Guildmembers have perfected, but the basic principles are these:

- If you're in the line of fire, find any cover you can. This might be an overturned table, a dead body, or even a decorative canopy. Blocking the shot is important, but blocking the shooter's line of sight is better than nothing.

- Find shot-stopping cover as quickly as you can. In an urban environment a parked speeder should keep you safe, unless your shooter has military-grade armament (or unless a stray shot punctures the fuel cells). The corner of a building is thicker than a single wall. Find someplace where you can pop your head out and make a quick check on enemy locations.
- When moving, stay low and run a zigzag pattern. Making yourself tough to hit is a lot more important than speed.
- Watch out for thrown explosives. Nothing will force you out of cover faster. If you have any thermal detonators, now's the time to use them.
- If you can, turn tail and run. Come back when you're better equipped—and make the kriffing barves pay for getting the drop on you. JETPACK IS USEFUL FOR QUICK ESCAPES. ALWAYS KEEP A RESERVE IN THE FUEL TANKS. BOBA

Don't pick flimsy cover. Your opponents can shoot right through it.

DISARMING AN ENEMY

When you get close to your target, you've got two priorities: make sure he can't kill you, and make sure he can't run. The first one's kind of important.

At brawling range there's no need to fire your blaster, but it's still a nice, heavy weight you can swing into the side of a target's head. Of course, your enemy will probably be armed, too. Even a hydrospanner can be used as a club, and somebody with training might be packing a vibro-sword or a force pike. There are even a few jet-juicers who carry light-sabers and pretend to be Jedi Knights. I knew a runner named Yadra Kunu who killed a hunter with a glass of water. *How did he do that? – Greedo*

Wielding a weapon extends your reach–your enemy's, too.

Don't focus on the weapon—focus on its radius and combat profile. A force pike cuts a wide arc to make you keep your distance, but a force pike can't be brought back into position as quickly as a short blade. If your enemy overextends his swing, close the distance and deliver a quick punch to the face.

If you've got a blade, use it. Keep your arm halfway extended and your weapon in a position to block up, down, left, and right. Strike with the middle of the blade, and hit hard. Always advance. Use short slashes, not lunging thrusts. You want to knock his weapon out of his hands, or cut the tendons of the arm that's holding it.

Forget fistfights. If your target has legs, break them.
- Bossk

GOING HAND-TO-HAND

Even if neither of you has weapons, you still might be looking at an old-fashioned fistfight. Keep it short. That fancy teras kasi stuff is only for the holovids. Meet a punch—don't back away—and you'll cut the blow's power by half. Block with your forearms. Try to take a punch in the forehead instead of the nose.

Species with skeletons have weak points in their limb joints and whatever they call their brain box. Punch hard and rattle their skull. Kick with power and snap their knee.

Put everything into your first punch. You might not get a second one.

Deliver a sufficiently brutal beatdown and your target won't be a threat anymore, and probably won't be able to run either. Time to snap on the magnacuffs. And unless you like scrubbing out bloodstains, lay down a tarp in your ship's hold first.

IMPROVISING A RIDE

The ride you use in the field doesn't have to be your own. If you're in a hurry, you can commandeer a vehicle, or simply "borrow" one.

Commandeer: On the Rim, licensed bounty hunters are authorized to seize civilian vehicles for temporary use in the pursuit of targets wanted for violent crimes. Just know that not every local badge will see it the same way.

While showing the driver your IPKC, announce in a clear voice that you're making use of their ride for a law enforcement emergency. And let them get out before you take the controls. After it's over, you'll have to compensate them for the hassle or for the cost of a wrecked vehicle.

"Borrow": It goes without saying that boosting a ride violates local laws, but a Guild hunter should weigh the risks and make an on-the-spot judgment call.

Start with a vehicle lot, which should have dozens of ready-to-drive landspeeders if you can get past the security gate. Here's the thing: with the rise of cheap descramblers, locks on Rim worlds are often metal or ceramic assemblies you open by depressing a sequence of pins and rotating a core cylinder. With practice and a memory-metal pick you can jigger it open.

DISCONNECT LEADS FROM THE SPARK STARTER AND HIT IT WITH A LOW POWER (0.050–0.080) BLASTER BURN. BoBA

Once you're inside, you can hotwire most landspeeders by sending a positive charge into the turbine grid and a second charge into the repulsorlift coil. Do this by crosswiring the central battery with these two components, and watch the speeder start itself. Study a wiring diagram first, for Edge's sake, unless you want to blow out the console or trigger the anti-theft irritants that will make your face puff up like a Huttlet's belly.

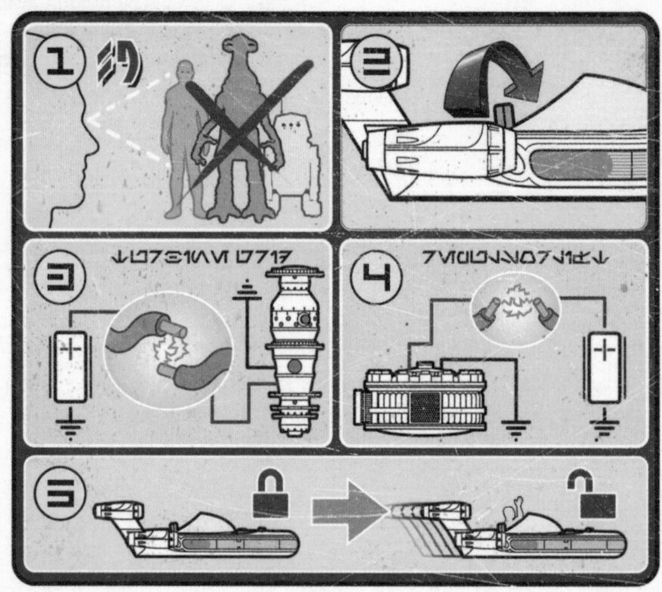

This hotwiring diagram is stenciled on the inside of your Guild vehicular toolkit (200 series and above).

BOARDING A MOVING SPEEDER FROM ANOTHER VEHICLE

This comes in handy more often than you'd think. Remember the basics:

- Set your autopilot. If you don't have one, or if you don't have a partner who can take over the controls after you jump, kiss your ride goodbye.
- Match altitude and speed. To prevent a last-second sideswipe by the target speeder, hang back one vehicle length. Gun the engine to pull up alongside, and plan to jump a moment after you let go of the throttle.
- Aim for an open window. Hopefully you've shattered at least one during the firefight leading up to this point.
- Push off with both feet and leap slightly ahead of the window, accounting for wind resistance and speed.
- Drag yourself inside, take out anybody who's armed, then go for the driver. If the driver puts the speeder into a violent turn, it might send you right back out the same way you came in.

I guess an open window would hurt less. Live and learn.
– Bossk

BAILING OUT OF A SPEEDER

If the driver is steering toward a collision (or if a blaster bolt accidentally fried the control panel), you might need to abandon a speeder while it's still moving. Here's what you need to know:

- Make sure your exit is clear. A rear hatch is the best choice, but if you're in a hurry you can shoot out the windscreen.
- Look for a place to make a low-impact landing. A clear downward slope is the best option. Water, snow, tall grass, or rotting garbage might work too.
- Jump as far away from the speeder as possible. Watch out that you don't get clipped by the rear engines or the tail assembly.

Falling? Slow your descent and aim for a miracle.

ybe I should
r a jetpack
the time,
in case.
Greedo

- You'll be moving at the same speed as the vehicle you just left, so tuck your limbs in close and bleed your momentum with a side-body roll. Ever wonder why some hunters wear armor that wouldn't stop a blaster bolt? This is why. Your armor will protect you from scrapes and punctures, and might absorb enough of the impact to keep you from popping a joint or losing a limb.

- If you're in an airspeeder at high altitude, keep your body splayed with your limbs and appendages extended for maximum drag. Orient yourself facedown and scan for vegetation canopies, deep snow masses, or spongy bog muck. Steer in that direction by leaning your shoulders. If the impact doesn't kill you it'll almost certainly shock you senseless, so hopefully an accomplice has been tracking your fall and can get you into a bacta tank fast.

BOARDING A HOVERTRAIN

On worlds with high-pressure atmospheres, like Quarzite, the locals move all crossplanet shipping with a network of subtrams running through vast subcrustal caverns. The Kage Warriors of Quarzite have their own techniques for raiding these transports, which should come in handy for any hunter needing to board a hovertrain:

- Match speed with the hovertrain, and come up alongside the joining of two train cars. The Kage Warriors use native mounts called milodons, but you can get the same effect with a speeder bike.

- Leap into the gap between the cars. Consider wearing magnetic gauntlets. If you slip, make a grab for the side rail.

- Climb to the top of your train car. You'll need to move up the entire length of the hovertrain, since valuables and VIP passengers are usually kept under guard in the cars immediately behind the engine.

- Lean into the wind and stay crouched as you move, using your hands for balance.

- Watch out for turns. Keep still during the direction shift and move forward when the train hits a straightaway.

- If the train enters a tunnel, drop flat on your stomach. For safety reasons you'll find that most tunnels are designed with at least a meter of clearance, but you don't want to be taking chances at 450 kilometers per hour.

Borokki makes jumping a hovertrain sound easy. Maybe she should try it while under attack by Kage Warriors. — Dengar

A hovertrain isn't tough to board if you match its speed first.

SURVIVING AN ANIMAL ATTACK

You might be armed to the gills, but most carnivores will still happily try to eat you. Whether you're in the forest, jungle, or desert, you can classify hostile animals into broad categories and figure out the best approach.

If It's Bigger Than You: Think rancor, acklay, or krayt dragon. You're already at a size disadvantage, so even the odds. If there's cover around, like a thick tree trunk or a pillar in a Hutt dungeon, maneuver to the opposite side and keep the beast at a distance where it can't use its claws or teeth. If you have a ranged weapon, go for the eyes or equivalent sensory organs.

ied the smoke
nade and the
arbine grease.
idn't work.
— Greedo

If that doesn't work, do everything you can to vanish from the monster's senses. Because most animals track by scent, you can mask your odor by emptying a smoke grenade inside your jacket or rubbing carbine grease on your skin. Or crack open a tin of rations and hurl it as far away from you as possible.

Still not helping? Drop to the ground and lie still. Don't run. You're not going to outrace it.

gainst
odian
ench?
f course
didn't!
Bossk

If you do get eaten you've still got one more shot. Take a deep breath before you slide down the thing's throat, and free your knife (or anything else that's sharp) before the swallowing reflex pins your arms to your side. Hold the blade out perpendicular to your body and drag it upwards. If you're lucky, the monster will spit you out. If not, keep holding your breath until you carve an "X" in its stomach big enough to push your head through.

If It's About Your Size: Think gundark, nexu, or gohai. Just because it's closer to your weight class doesn't mean it'll be any easier to take down.

First things first: Don't go mistaking a threat display for an actual threat. A low growl, a waving stinger, or an extended frill are just warnings, and you might be able to get out of trouble with no fighting at all. Back away slowly, out of whatever perimeter the creature considers its territory. Try

Gohai are common in the wilds of the Expansion Region. If a gohai charges, hit the deck.

not to stink too much. And don't go striding around, all jingle-jangle in polished metal armor. They're still picking pieces of Elevan the Boastful out of the roc aeries on Skye.

If the danger's real, it makes a difference whether you're about to be jumped by a single animal or a pack. If you think it's the latter, run for a chokepoint like a treetop or a narrow-mouthed cave. The members of the pack will be forced to face you one on one.

Against a single predator, you can sometimes bluff your way out of a jam if the beast isn't too bright. Wave a cape or cloak to make your body's silhouette look bigger than it actually is, or throw stones to show you're not defenseless. You can also shout at the animal, but only in a low register. A high-pitched squeak is the universal sound of wounded prey. If you're a Chadra-Fan, keep your snout shut.

If the beast leaps at you, pull it into a grapple. Hook one arm around its neck to cut off its air supply. If it's aquatic jab it in the gills. Shift your weight so you stay on top of it, on its back. Do everything you can to keep any claws on the ground or pinned down so they're not scrabbling at your guts. Some vac-brained animals like globblins will calm down if you cover their eyes.

Most animals that hunt live prey will go for a deep neck bite to bleed out or suffocate their victim, or a bite and a violent head-shake to snap the spinal column. If the creature gets the upper hand, curl up to protect your vital organs and shield your neck with your arms.

If It's Smaller Than You: Tiny buggers might be the last thing you'll ever see, especially if they're venomous or attack in swarms. Think botflies, scurriers, or vrelts. If you're poisoned, see BHG supplemental 7-87: *Poisons, Venoms, and Antidotes* for emergency treatment.

If you're facing a swarm, a wrist-mounted flamethrower will lay down a perimeter burn that will make them keep their distance. The same trick works with smoke or aerosol toxins. Even a paint-tagger is better than nothing, because fumes like that are repulsive to most animals and can be ignited with a spark. Just don't try that on Skako or any other planet with a dense methane atmosphere.

- TOO MUCH FLAME IN A CONFINED SPACE CAN IGNITE SECONDARY EXPLOSIONS. WATCH OUT FOR FUEL CELLS. BOBA

To escape from a swarm, look for cover in high grasses or try to get inside anything that has a door. Diving into water might work if you've got a submersible breather and can stay down there for a while. If not, you'll have to fight it out on the water's surface with a horde of swimming, biting, scratching vermin. Don't believe me? Next time you're at the Sriluur Guildhouse, ask Ojoon "Half-Face" Coi how he got his name.

Keep your flame low for better precision.

CRASH LANDING, AND SURVIVING WHEN MAROONED

Membership in the Bounty Hunters Guild comes with benefits beyond the training, the expediting, and even the access to rare gear. It also entitles you to the Guild's protection. On your first hunt you'll receive encrypted Guildhouse frequencies and emergency beacons that alert nearby Guildmembers if one of their own is in severe distress.

And by "severe distress" we mean crashing on an uncharted planet with your ship full of holes, not bumping your head on the cargo ramp. A crash is one of the worst things a spacer can face, but it's exactly the kind of situation where the Guild can save your hide.

Remember these tips:

- Call for help on the Guild's hypercom and subspace frequencies before you slip into the planet's gravity well. After that point, atmospheric and gravitic interference will jam the signal.
- Most starships don't have airfoils, so don't count on gliding to a landing. You'll need to balance your forward thrust and the lift from your antigrav repulsors to keep your ship from dropping like a rock.
- Stay level as you shed altitude. Look for a large body of water or a wide, flat plain. Don't lower your landing gear—it'll just snag and break.
- Strap yourself into the cockpit's crash webbing.
- After the impact, punch the Guild emergency beacon on the control panel as soon as the ship has settled.
- If the ship has suffered a reactor breach, or you've landed on water and the ship isn't seaworthy, take a smaller Guild beacon with you and get some distance between you and the wreckage.

Now your job is to stay alive. Pickup could take hours or weeks, depending on how far you are from the major spacelanes.

It doesn't matter if you've landed in the desert or atop a glacier, and it makes little difference if you're a human or a Patrolian. Your first task is

Stay with the wreck if you can. It offers shelter and easy identification from the air.

to find drinkable water. If your ship is still intact, take as much water with you as you can carry, draining the fluidic lines if necessary. If you have a portable hydro-extractor with you, you'll be able to purify any liquid you come across in the wild, even when there's a rotted animal carcass bobbing in it. A hydro-extractor can also pull water out of dry air like a moisture condenser, but don't count on it to produce anything more than a few swallows.

If you're going to be traveling over land, hike up a ridge to get a view of the surrounding terrain. Then head downslope. You're more likely to find water underneath gravel washes, or to find colonist settlements at river mouths. Look for where bird flocks and gasbag floaters are circling, because it might be a coastline.

Find a big stick. It'll make hiking easier, can help keep wild animals at bay, and will help you push your way free from protoplasmic mires. Don't travel during midday in hot zones, or after dark in cold ones. You can start a fire by switching your blaster to its lowest power setting and keeping the trigger squeezed, but if you're in hostile country the smoke might attract unwanted attention.

Notify Rebel Command about bounty hunter rescue signals.
— Han Solo

If you see what looks like a rescue ship overhead, signal it with your blaster. Two shots, then a pause, then two more shots.

Remember that your Guildmates are here to back you up, but they're not suckers. They deserve to be well paid for saving your life. Once you've recovered, a Guild contractor will go over the plan and timetable under which you'll compensate the Guild for destroyed equipment and the loss of hours diverted from hunt operations.

PATCHING WOUNDS

Hunting on the galactic fringe doesn't give you many chances to enjoy a clean bed or a good meal. And you can forget about finding a decent doc. On one run to Ord Vaxal, my partner, Nirittu Kotta, went under the knife with a rusted DD-13 surgical droid the planetary sheriff kept in her storage shed. He limped in with a knife wound in his thigh, and 10 minutes later he hopped out a whole leg lighter. You can skip this kind of frontier butchery if you learn to stabilize injuries long enough to reach a medcenter where people know what they're doing.

Shot with a blaster: The big question is how deep the other guy got you. A glancing hit with a blaster bolt will cause skin burns and tissue damage from the ionized plasma, but no blood loss. Stop it from becoming infected by peeling melted armor plating away from the wound (don't be stupid and peel away your flesh) and wrapping it with a sterile dressing like HapTex, or at least a clean length of cloth.

Apply a kolto patch if you've got one, as kolto is better than bacta at regenerating burned tissue. And take a little something for the pain. Renan Irongut is my favorite pain reliever that's bottled at a distillery.

A deeper shot means you've got bleeding to worry about. A blaster bolt won't cauterize a deep wound, so an Aqualish will bleed out in minutes. Try to stop it with direct pressure or by pinching off an artery pressure point. If the hit's in a limb, a drastic option is a tourniquet (a cloth wrap and a stick that you turn like a crank to tighten the wrap). It'll create so much pressure that the blood flow will stop completely, but you might lose the limb too. Unless you're a Trandoshan. Those lucky re-gens save a fortune on cyborg parts.

Mechasomes are losers. - Bossk

The Skine cantina. They resurface the walls every month.

Speared or stabbed: Follow the same steps for treating a deep blaster wound—that is, unless you've still got the weapon sticking out of your body. If an arrow or a dagger is staying put, it's also probably holding your guts together.

This is why vibroweapons are so deadly. That humming blade edge keeps cutting as long as the power cell holds out. The Guildmembers on Skine used to drive their vibroknives into the top of the cantina wall when they went out drinking, and the one with the knife that had traveled the shortest distance after the third or fourth round had to pick up the tab.

Anyway, don't try pulling a standard weapon out of your body if there's a chance it pierced a vital organ. Break it off near the skin if you can, then keep the stub from moving with a tight wrap. A decently stocked medkit will have a canister of plasto spray, which you can also use as a bandage.

Broken limb: Whether you have an endoskeleton or an exoskeleton, if you get a fracture on a load-bearing limb, you're probably out of the hunt.

Immobilize the break to keep the broken ends from grinding against each other. Make a couple long, straight splints. You can use big sticks, HoloNet antennas, whatever. Tie them tightly in place against the limb.

You can make a cast out of plasto spray if you empty the whole can at once. And if your ship has a medbay, you might even find a Sluissi gravitic pressure bandage, which uses microrepulsors to stabilize the entire cross-section of the injured limb and prevent any internal bleeding.

If you don't have time to waste on healing, the Verpine make something called a carapace knitter. It's a calcium paste that sets into a molecular glue once it's out of the tube, and will crudely mend a bone in about five minutes. The problem is, it's made for insectoids. If you want to stitch up a bone inside a flesh cocoon, you need to inject the calcium paste. It hurts like hell, so take *two* swigs of the Irongut first.

Careful with the carapace knitter. Use too much and you'll kill the limb.

Poisoned: Brightly colored critters sometimes pack chemical weapons. An animal might inject poison with a bite, or shoot toxic quills that break the skin. Or it might spit globs of poison that get absorbed into your pores, or maybe even exhale a miasma that fogs your mouth and nostrils.

If you've been poisoned and if you're alone, run through these steps:

- Even if you've killed the thing that got you, get away. It might have a mate, or it could reflexively bite you again during its death spasms.
- If you've swallowed or inhaled the poison, try to vomit up the contents of your gut. Sniffing the flash powder out of your blaster's waterseal cap might help clear your airways.
- If the bite is on one of your limbs, keep the limb low, below your heart. Avoid strenuous movements that get the blood pumping.
- Wrap the limb with a pressure bandage between your heart and the bite location. That Sluissi gravitic bandage and its microrepulsors would be perfect here.
- If you think the poison might be from a fire wasp, cut into the wound and fish around until you find the stinger. You really don't want the egg pod embedded in the stinger to hatch. And don't forget: fire wasps aren't the only things that reproduce this way.
- If the wound starts to swell, remove your armor. I once saw a Mandalorian allergic to blisterbug venom who refused to take off his breastplate in the name of Mando'a honor. He's the first guy I ever saw get suffocated by stubbornness.

NOTE: INVESTIGATE COST AND EFFECTIVENESS OF ELF-STABLE ANTI-INFLAMMATORIES.
BOBA

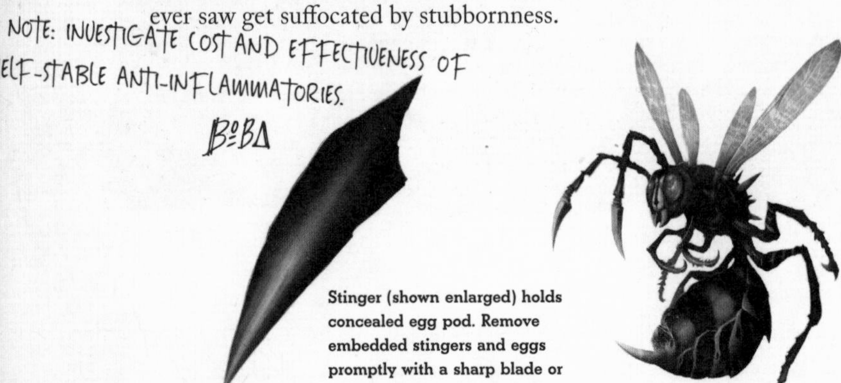

Stinger (shown enlarged) holds concealed egg pod. Remove embedded stingers and eggs promptly with a sharp blade or laser scalpel.

This info should be on your datapad, but it wouldn't hurt to memorize it.

TOOLS OF THE TRADE

BY CHENTU CHEK,

ARMORY MASTER, 23-YEAR VETERAN OF THE GUILD

What you carry is as important as what you know. Don't set out on a job until you've restocked your supply bag. And here's some advice from an old hand: every time you collect money from a bounty, you should reinvest part of your payment into new gear. The Guild will also rent or lease specialty equipment. Good gear can't make a bad hunter good, but bad gear's a burden on any hunter, even you.

For some hunts, your contractor will make suggestions before you set out. On an aquatic run to Mon Cala, for example, you'll need an air tank, a nitrogen purger, and a harpoon gun. A hotfoot chase through the calderas of Magmar will go wrong unless you're carrying a narrow-band spectral filter and a composite armor suit that's been furnace-tested to 1,700 degrees. You can sign out specialized gear from a Guildhouse armorer, but any damage will be subtracted from your deposit. If you break it, all you can do is hope the bounty you earn is enough to turn your trip into a net profit. Better yet, don't break it.

Your gear should suit the hunt and fit your style. What you'll find in this section are only samples to give you a starting point. For a deep dive, refer to BHG supplemental 2-02: *Guildhouse Armory Inventory*.

TRACKING DEVICES

There's risk-versus-reward to consider when it comes to trackers, and it's something hunters love to argue about. On the one side, let's say the tracker gets discovered, or you tag the wrong ship. Well then, you just wasted a pile of credits. On the other side, if the tracer works, you can almost skip the entire Evaluation phase and happily trail your target all the way out to the wisps of the Tingel Arm.

Tracking devices are also known as homing beacons or bugs, and they work by sending their signals on the same faster-than-light S-thread channels that make up the HoloNet. Even in hyperspace, a secure tracker can secretly send a blink to the nearest non-mass transceiver, allowing you to fix the bug's location down to the sector or system level. And once you've emerged from hyperspace in the same area, you can pin the signal down even more precisely by switching over to subspace frequencies.

XX-23 portable mode (left) and deployed

High End: The Neuro-Savv XX-23 is a tracker that can take a beating and keep on beeping. If you shoot it onto a starship's hull, it will attach with a nearly unbreakable molecular bond. Plus, when the target ship's engines are active the tracker will power itself off of the heat and radiation emissions. This makes the XX-23 almost impossible to detect with a standard anti-bugging scan. This unit goes for 4,400 credits and, yes, you have to buy your own. The Guild can't afford to loan these out when there's a decent risk they won't be recovered.

Low End: Tracking doesn't have to stop when your target goes dirtside. Unless you're one of those tracks-and-twigs types who can follow a target by looking at a bent blade of grass, think about buying a surface tracer like the Astroserver Rover (1,000 credits). It can be clamped to a landspeeder or hidden inside a cargo pouch. Wherever it goes, it will use EM frequencies to broadcast its range, speed, and direction right to your handheld receiver.

Maybe somee
at Jabba's c
get me a de
on a Rover.
– Greedo

SURVEILLANCE GEAR

Sometimes you don't need to follow a target, but you still want to know what they're cooking up. Me, I like to slip a few creds to the bartender, who's probably overheard plenty. But if you like to go sneakier when solving your problems, take a look at these:

High End: The Loronar Fly Eye (1,400 credits) is a recording device with a tiny repulsorlift engine and four claws that grip walls and ceilings. Once it's in position, you can listen in by tuning to the right frequency on your earpiece. Because the Fly Eye is a dead giveaway if it's spotted, some prefer Arakyd's Moon Moth. This thing is basically an insect droid packed with Fly Eye hardware, running a movement subroutine that makes it flutter overhead and bash itself into glow lanterns. It's also got a threat detector to keep it out of swatting reach and protect your 2,800-credit investment. If you buy one, don't get so excited that you forget to make it look native. The Moon Moth's programmable wings can go from Socorran sand-brown to Felucian phosphorescent.

Loronar's Fly Eye (left) and Arakyd's Moon Moth

Low End: Down in the cellars of many Guildhouses, past the cases of Whyren's Reserve and the empty bottles of Gizer ale, down where the light doesn't reach and the water drips from the walls, is where you'll find the mimbranes. Pick one of them out of its crevice and you've got yourself a free and nearly undetectable listening device. The Guild discovered these noise-feeders on the Q'nithian moon, and since then they've been smartly cultivating colonies of their own. Drop a mimbrane close to your target and it'll absorb all sound. When you squeeze it later, it'll spit up everything it "ate" in a perfect audio playback. Because the mimbrane is an animal (or maybe a plant—I'm not an expert) it's got no electronic components to show up on anti-bugging scans. But you won't get any pictures out of it, and a mimbrane's captured soundscape is sometimes so muddy you can't make out individual voices. And, fair warning—if a hungry Skrilling sniffs one out he'll swallow it whole.

Mimbranes are as unreliable as they are cheap.
— Dengar

A Q'nithian mimbrane is practically undetectable.

DATA SLICING TOOLS

Most of the research you do during the Evaluation phase of the hunt is completely legal and relatively safe. The work you do in the field? Not so much. Computers can make information retrieval a lot less risky, and luckily they all have a fatal flaw: their interface port. A computer that can be jacked is a computer that can be cracked.

A droid can plug in to an interface port with its scomp-link arm, and you can do the same thing with a code cylinder. Now, a computer guarding valuable secrets might have a socketguard countermeasure, which will shunt electrical current into your device and maybe make it explode. But if you can get past the authentication screen and inside the computer network, you'll have some real power right there at your fingers. You can shut down power grids, tap into observation feeds, trip alarms, copy data records, or even make a really big boom by overloading the fusion reactor.

High End: If you want a more subtle approach, give some thought to a slicer droid. R2 units and other astromechs can sometimes feel their way through security networks (in addition to plotting your hyperspace jumps and calibrating your power couplings). But astromechs aren't built to be slicers. Check the MerenData product catalog instead, where you'll see plenty of options, most of them guaranteed against catastrophic socketguard failure. The top of the line is MerenData's B2-X. This positronic processor fits in a palm-sized shell, so it can be carried on your belt or hidden in plain sight as a component of a larger piece of equipment. If you plug a B2-X into an interface port it will baffle its way through anything including a Mandalmatrix encryption screen. MerenData only manufactures the B2-X on an order-by-order basis, and one of them will set you back nearly 60,000 credits.

Low End: Data spikes are a smart choice if you're more of a fighter than a byter. Spikes cause a one-time overload by flooding the system with junk data, and they cost about 1,500 credits each. Spikes are a brute-force way to get inside a network, but they'll do permanent damage to the terminal and make your tampering so obvious a blind gussul could see it.

BL-17 WAS COMPETENT AND VERSATILE. GET NEW DROID AFTER MECHIS JOB. BoBA

REPULSORLIFT SPEEDERS

Once you've tracked your target to solid ground, you'll want to scout the terrain and follow up on leads. You might also need to chase down a runner, or even escape from a mob that's howling for your blood. If you've got your own speeder, you've got it covered.

But which speeder? Airspeeder, landspeeder, or speeder bike? Aside from the obvious—go with what you can afford—you've got to consider what you can carry. And what can carry *it*. A speeder bike can fit aboard even a small freighter if you hook it to the ceiling with magnetic clamps. But an airspeeder? Forget about it.

No matter which type of speeder you wind up with, you should spend a lot more time upgrading it than you did picking it out. Both airspeeders and landspeeders have enough bulk on their frames to support at least two things from this list:

- Magnetic harpoon
- Laser cutter
- Hull-rending buzz saw
- Cargo-strength tractor beam
- Concussion missile launcher (with linear and spread firing patterns)
- 8,000-volt anti-tampering system
- Front-mounted bantha wedge
- "Silent running" engine dampeners
- Electrified Conner net launcher
- Stokhli adhesive sprayer
- Smoke screen sprayer
- Tracking device scrambling field
- White Dwarf high-beam floodlights

I'd want all these on my speeder.
– Greedo

I saw Greedo fall off a speeder twice. And it was parked!
- Bossk

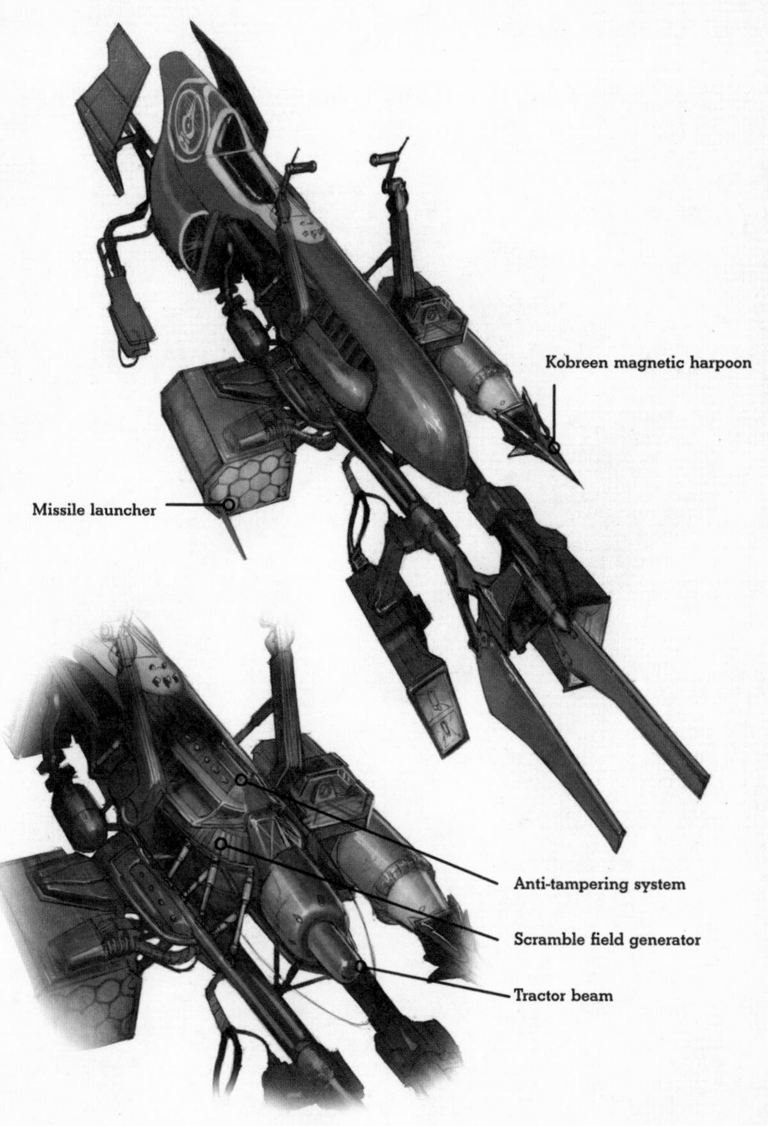

A speeder with the right upgrades: improved, but not overloaded

AIRSPEEDERS

Unless you're cruising around in a star yacht, you probably don't have enough room in your hold for an airspeeder. But if you do, an airspeeder's enclosed cockpit and extended range make it a handy mobile HQ for planet-side operations.

Incom T-47 (top) and Orbitblade 2000. A nose-mounted concussion missile is standard on Zzip's aerospace transport.

High End: The Orbitblade 2000 from Zzip is so new you'll probably need to order it direct from the factory (expect to pay in the neighborhood of 120,000 credits). It has a top speed of 1,050 kph, and comes with a concussion missile launcher and mounts for modular installation of whatever else you have in mind. Its armor is comparable to the T-47, but its cockpit is environmentally sealed, so no worries about poisonous vapors even when you're hunting on Drackmar.

Low End: Incom's T-47 is a standard cargo-moving model, which is why you can find a used one for under 6,500 credits. It has a top speed of 650 kph, and its chassis can stand up to whatever you throw at it. So many

Those cocky kids racing their T-47s at Beggars Canyon would make good target practice.
— Greedo

T-47s on the used market have a pair of forward-facing blaster cannons, you'd swear they come standard. The T-47 is technically a two-person airspeeder, but the second seat is only there for somebody to work the cargo towline. Most hunters rip out the extra seat and replace it with a storage locker or restraint cage.

LANDSPEEDERS

You lose an entire axis of movement by going down to a landspeeder, because its repulsorlifts only give a vertical boost of a meter or so. But overland traveling is good enough nine hunts out of ten, and if your trail takes you to Cloud City you can always rent an airspeeder.

The MandalMotors BAX-7 (top) and SoroSuub's V-35

LANDSPEEDER REPAIRS AND UPGRADES:
- TAMJA GARAGE, SOCORRO: INSTALLED U-TRIP 22SX AFTERBURNERS
- STALGASIN HIVE, GEONOSIS: INSTALLED HOOD-MOUNTED SONIC CANNON
- PORT WHISPER, VONTOR: MECHANIC FOUND SOURCE OF PERSISTENT RATTLE AND KILLED IT

BOBA

High End: MandalMotors has cranked out some nice rides, but credit-for-credit the LUX-3 is the better investment. It's sealed up tight like the Orbitblade, and it can hover three meters off the ground unusually high for a landspeeder, and good enough to vault over plenty of obstacles. The LUX-3's best assets are its twin jet turbines, which give it a top speed of 620 kph. It's also got predictive terrain-following sensors that give you what seems like a precog's awareness of upcoming trouble. The LUX-3 is 80,000 credits new, but the Guild has a motor pool of missile-equipped models at the Guildhouses on Tatooine, Terminus, and Port Haven. Start one up, and it's like somebody just waved the starting flag at a Podrace.

Low End: SoroSuub's V-35 Courier is so common nobody gives it a second glance. They're everywhere, so they're practically invisible. A used V-35 can go for 1,500 creds, and a morning spent tinkering with aftermarket parts will really juice its 120 kph max speed. Because the Courier's driver/passenger compartment is enclosed, you can replace the plastic canopy with one made of tinted transparisteel and turn your bargain-basement ride into a blasterproof tank.

SPEEDER BIKES

Most hunters come into the Guild with at least some experience riding swoops. You know, illegal races, and maybe a few brushes with the law. But listen up: swoop bikes are unbalanced, and are all about speed and style instead of reliable performance. Go for a custom-built speeder bike instead of a chop-shop swoop or you'll look like some Rimmer punk.

Rimmer punk, huh? Chentu Chek an
I will hav to have a little talk about that.
– Dengar

High End: Ikas-Adno has been in the speeder market for centuries, and the 88-R Nightscreamer might be the best thing their craftserfs have ever knocked together. Its top speed is a suicidal 750 kph, and it generates a forward-facing particle shield that deflects wind and grit, and it will even nudge you away from glancing collisions. The Nightscreamer starts at 11,500 credits, and a standard aftermarket package will add a low-slung twin blaster cannon and a rear-mounted shrapnel cloud emitter. Punch that shrapnel cloud when you've got a baddie glued to your tail, and I swear you'll never again underestimate the effect of metal fragments in the face. The Nightscreamer also allows installation of a sidecar, which can be handy for carrying your slicer droid or transporting a trussed-up acquisition.

Low End: The 74-Z is Aratech's old reliable. It's the bike of choice for Imperial scout troopers, and the military model comes with a single forward-facing blaster cannon. Military models are easy to get on the invisible market for as little as 1,800 credits, what with all the Squibs scavenging them from battlefields and fixing them up. Its top speed is a handy 500 kph but it offers zero protection against blaster bolts or flying insects. For those of you who barely have two creds to rub together, you can scrounge up cheap parts from a Clone Wars–era BARC speeder bike and assemble your own for next to nothing.

To accommodate humanoids of differing sizes, Aratech makes many options available for controls, thrusters, and repulsorlift power on the 74-Z speeder bike.

TARGET TRAPPERS

These items can turn the odds in your favor if you're tracking a runner or a hider. You'll find that a careful trap is often more important than a big blaster.

Tangler guns are great for taking down runners.

Tangler gun: Great for stopping a fleeing target but pretty useless in an actual firefight, the Salus tangler gun should find a place in your gear bag only when you go after bounties who aren't likely to have backup. A tangler gun will set you back about 900 credits and fires three linked lengths of weighted durawire. If your shot connects, the whole bundle will wrap tightly around the target.

Net shooter: This gives you a wider area of effect than the tangler gun. The explosive-release nets (about 200 credits each) are packed into grenade casings, meaning you can load them into pretty much any standard-bore launcher. Fire it above your target, not *at* your target, unless you want the grenade's impact to knock them off their feet before the net can deploy.

Man trap: This one's nice since it immobilizes without immediate injury. Ubrikkian makes one that costs 8,000 credits. The man trap is a one-meter-square metal plate embedded with gravfield generators that amplify the local gravity up to ten times. When somebody steps onto the plate, they're yanked to the dirt and pinned until you come to collect them. Just don't take all day. Too long under a man trap and your target's organs will start leaking.

Bio-cocoon: Here's one trap that genuinely gives me the shivers. It's a square plastic sheet saturated with an inert culture of kivilol spores. With a footstep, those specks get kicked out of dormancy. In seconds they've reproduced two, four, eight, sixteen times, and before you can blink, a crawling mass of the microscopic things are creeping up the target's leg, eating away as they go. The poor sucker will be dead in under a minute, so retrieve him fast. You can buy a bio-cocoon from Dendratis Exports for 2,000 credits, but remember: the bio-cocoon is a restricted biological hazard. You'll have to pay over and over, every time you bribe your way through customs.

If you don't use the bio-cocoon within a year its cultures will die off.

Motion sensor array: If your target's holed up, you'll want to know when they finally decide to make a break for it. Setting up a motion sensor array is cheap and easy, and a half-dozen sensors will project an invisible web that's sensitive to vibrations. You can calibrate it so it won't flag every grainfly that buzzes past, but that means it won't work too well in urban settings—you'll be spending all day chasing street beggars and service droids. Neuro-Savv makes a good set that's a bargain at about 50 creds.

CROWD CONTROL

Weapons that hit lots of people at once are questionable choices for bounty hunters. They're indiscriminate, and hunters should think "pick 'em off" not "mow 'em down." But if you're going to be boarding a lot of starships, they can come in handy.

Pulse rifle: The Corondexx VES-700 (a pricey 5,000 credits) releases hundreds of tiny ion bursts in a 60-degree arc with each shot. These ion firings will overload electronics and overwhelm biological nervous systems. The superconducting filaments in the barrel of the Corondexx are a nightmare to maintain, and in time you might find yourself sinking as much into keeping the thing fixed as you did buying it in the first place.

Deck-sweeper: If you're set on crowd control but can't afford the pulse rifle, Merr-Sonn's deck-sweeper is the basic, wide-beam stun blaster for you. It fires in a 45-degree arc to a range of about five meters. Anyone outside the narrow firing cone won't fall down unconscious, but narrow starship corridors have a way of herding your enemies into blasting range. Merr-Sonn manufactures the deck-sweeper for Imperial riot police, but you can find them on the invisible market for 500 credits each.

Flechette launcher: This is a military anti-personnel weapon pumped out by Golan Arms for the planetary militias in the Western Reaches. There are plenty available for as little as 800 credits, but I wouldn't bother unless you're planning to do a whole lot of killing. This thing's flechette canisters burst into a spray of microdarts, and if that doesn't sound so bad then you've never seen the carnage a flechette strike at close range can unleash. Pick your battles carefully and remember that bounty hunters shouldn't cause more damage than necessary. Leave that kind of thing to the pirates and slavers.

ABC scrambler: An ABC scrambler outdoes a flash grenade in every possible way. Once it goes off it emits a disorienting ultrasonic shriek and releases a cloud of chemical irritants. Depending on what kinds of organs your target uses to navigate, he might stagger around in a circle or fall to

UPDATED ARMOR'S ABC COUNTERMEASURES,
PLUS REDUNDANT BACKUPS. BOBA

his knees and vomit up his lunch. The ABC stands for "aural, biological, and chemical," and you get your money's worth with all three. Loronar offers these in grenade form for 500 credits a pop.

Glop grenade: Merr-Sonn makes these for the Corporate Sector so the Espo goons there can round up anti-company protestors before cracking their skulls. Lots of glop grenades are quietly sold on the side, and you can pick up a single G-20 for about 275 credits. Upon exploding, it sprays adhesive foam that solidifies in seconds.

There's nothing li
lighting u
Espos wit
their own
grenades.
— Dengar

A target with fur isn't going to like the cleanup from a glop grenade, but that's not your problem.

Here's what a doubler suit does. If you can get it to work.

DEFENSE ITEMS

You could write a whole book about armor (and we did: see BHG supplemental 2-04: *Guildhouse Armor Options and Configurations*), so here are a few other defensive options you might not have known existed. I'm not a big fan of some of these, so keep the opinion of a veteran hunter in mind as you browse these choices.

Stun cloak: You can tell when somebody's wearing a stun cloak by the glint of the metallic fibers in the weave. It electrostatically clings to living skin, so if you touch one you'll be flapping your arm around wildly trying to make it let go. And that's when the wearer activates the electric charge and zaps you clean out of your boots. Koromondian makes a

One of Jabba's Gamorreans took mine, but I'll get it back. — Greedo three-charge cloak that costs 1,500 credits. Maybe I've had one too many bad encounters, but I swear I'd like to line up every one of the company's designers and punch them in the teeth.

Doubler suit: I'm no techhunter, so when I look at the doubler suit I see everything that's gone wrong with our proud art. Corellidyne's doubler suit uses a holovid recorder and projector to copy your image and beam a holographic doppelgänger somewhere else, all in the hope of drawing enemy fire. For the 30,000 credits this thing costs, you could buy 200 rounds of explosive ammo, 50 cases of Savareen brandy, or a long weekend in the bathhouses of Nuswatta. And any one of those will have more impact on your hunting game than these toys.

Stun baton: Who wouldn't want a sturdy club that releases a low-powered stun charge every time you hit someone with it? It's perfect for keeping company at arm's length. There's also a bonus in the fact that—since Merr-Sonn makes these for planetary police forces—you're authorized to carry one as an IPKC-licensed law officer. The 300 credit price tag is almost worth it solely for the fact that you'll never have trouble with it at starport customs.

RANGED WEAPONS

Every hunter needs one, since every hunter needs to take long-distance shots. But there's a lot of difference between a blaster and a dart shooter. Take a look through the following samples.

Blaster rifle: You've probably already found a blaster rifle that suits your style, so consider a hybrid rig if you're looking for more firepower. You can easily mount a microgrenade launcher below the barrel of most rifles, to give you a massive kick without needing to switch between weapons. The pump-action launcher uses magnetic propulsion to send grenades in 200-meter arcs. For an all-in-one model right off the assembly line, go with the Prax Arms "Blast & Smash" AXM-50 for 4,500 credits. New grenade magazines will cost an additional 1,000 credits a pop.

GOOD BALANCE OF FIREPOWER, ACCURACY, AND WEIGHT:
- EE-3 CARBINE RIFLE
- FIRESTAR 10-K
- MERR-SONN SCALPHUNTER

BOBA

A heavy blaster can be cumbersome, but you'll appreciate its greater firepower.

Heavy blaster pistol: If you're looking to upgrade the blaster pistol you're already packing, then BlasTech's Thunderer T-6 is a big chunk of deadly that's been cranked way above its safety limits. It's 750 credits from the manufacturer, but it's worth it for the intimidation factor alone. Set a Thunderer down when you take a seat at the bar and not even the drunken Abyssin is going to pick a fight.

Hold-out blaster: A concealed blaster pistol like this might save your life. It's small enough to be concealed in a boot, up a sleeve, or behind your back, and it could be your last line of defense against the goon who's pointing a weapon at your head. Merr-Sonn's Quickfire (650 credits) will fit into your palm but packs the same punch as a full-sized blaster pistol. And that's the catch. Because the Quickfire's power pack is strong enough to show up on weapons scans, you might need to swap it out for a one- or two-shot pack with an energy signature that's barely detectible.

If disruptors are stupid, how come Boba Fett uses a Zenloss DXR-4? – Greedo

Disruptor pistol: Disruptors rip apart organic tissue at the molecular level and are illegal on every planet in the Empire. I don't care if you're looking to kill, capture, or what—a disruptor is a stupid sidearm for a bounty hunter because it doesn't leave identifiable remains. I've never seen a client who'll pay for a box of ashes. Don't buy one, and don't ask where you can buy one. It'll only lead to heartache.

IT'S A DXR-6, NOT A 4, AND THE GUILD ARMORER'S THE STUPID ONE.

BOBA

Slugthrower rifle: Blasters usually win out over bullets, but there are still a few instances where you should choose an old-fashioned slugthrower over a modern blaster rifle. Say, when you need to sneak a rifle past a weapons scanner. Or when your target's estate is protected by energy shields but not particle shields. Just be sure you don't go *too* old-fashioned. Consider something like the Prax Arms HB-4. This 1,500-credit projectile rifle has a one-kilometer range and stays linked to its bullet with a short-burst, tight-beam transmission. The rig feeds directional data to the bullet after you fire it, so as long as you keep the bad guy in your crosshairs you're almost guaranteed a kill shot. Which is good, because the HB-4 isn't designed for rapid fire, and it's doubtful you'll have time to reload it.

Sometimes the basics are best.

Neural inhibitor: It costs a lot to own one (5,000 for the Mennotor 430, plus 750 creds for the ammo), but being able to paralyze your targets from long range could be worth the investment. A neural inhibitor fires darts loaded with neurotoxins that shut down a target's muscle control for about ten minutes. Many Guildhouses will let you rent out the ones in their armories, but unless you have a sniper's accuracy you might not be ready for the challenge.

SPECIALTY EQUIPMENT

Some stuff isn't categorized so easily but could still mean the difference between a successful hunt and a complete bust. This is just the beginning of the kinds of pieces you can collect if you've got the credits.

Force cage: I hope you don't think you can restrain your merchandise with nothing more than a pair of magnacuffs. A force cage doesn't take up much room, since you can collapse its ceramic frame and store it. Assembled, a force cage forms a cell four meters tall by two meters wide, with an energy field projected across the empty spaces in the frame to deliver a nasty shock to anyone foolish enough to touch it from the inside. Damorind Securities makes a popular one for around 7,000 credits. A word of warning: some species, like the Parwan, have bioelectric auras that let them push their way through, as long as they can stand the pain. Truss them up extra tight.

A collapsible, inexpensive force cage can pay for itself on your first job.

Line thrower: Scaling walls is only one of the things you can do with a good line thrower. Try stringing a cord between two buildings to move silently from rooftop to rooftop, or use its pulley system as a makeshift winch for hauling up heavy loads. I once knew a Selkath who speared game fish with a spiked grapple and hauled them back to shore with

GAUNTLET-FIRED WHIPCORD ACHIEVES THE SAME FUNCTION. LENGTH OF WHIPCORD A PROBLEM. CARRY CABLE SPOOL IN BELT POUCH? WEIGHT OKAY? BOBA the attached wire. The Susuax Verti-Go line thrower is only 400 credits, and comes with a variety of grappling heads including magnetic and molecular-adhesive. Its gas-fired launcher is a little noisier than I'd like, and its ascent motor screeches like a Sneevel—but that's no excuse for not having one of these in your field kit.

Squib battering ram: No, it's not made by the trash-scavenging Squibs, thank space. Fegegrish Heavy Industrials named their molecular ram after the furry thieves because Squibs can find their way inside anything that's not quadruple-locked. Clamp the business end of the ram against a door or wall, and its modulated energy pulses will weaken the internal makeup. When the indicator light glows green, haul back and swing the ram as hard as you can. Don't forget to back away from the hole you just made if you think your enemy might respond with blaster fire. This is an expensive piece at 3,500 credits, and it's backbreakingly heavy to boot.

Ultrasonic sight enhancer: We're not all born into the same species, and we don't all have the same gifts. You can either whine about it or do something to even the odds. Gotals, for example, can sense a whole universe of electromagnetics with their head cones. I knew a Gotal who lost both eyes to a Jubba bird, and he could still follow a flitgnat in a rainstorm. So can you if you drop 12,500 credits on an ultrasound painter like the one from Traxes Bioelectronics. It measures high-frequency sonic signatures and renders them as three-dimensional images in your occipital lobe (or whatever your visual neural cluster might be). Cost of implant surgery not included.

Voice scrambler: This little trinket throws up an audio block against eavesdroppers and looks like a piece of jewelry. The 600-credit model from Ulkop Securities projects a low-frequency distortion field up to three meters that makes your voice a muddled mess to any organic or electronic recorder outside the bubble. This thing won't work against telepaths, but then again not many Hortek survived the Imperial Navy's extermination order against their homeworld, so they're not exactly players anymore.

Repulsorboots: Maybe you're a risk taker with a high tolerance for broken bones. Well, these things are just what they sound like—boots with antigrav coils in the soles. Balance is a big problem with them, and it's easy to slide out of control like a pinwheeling rocketsled on a frozen lake. But repulsorboots can be useful for skipping over stretches of swampy muck, and the Nimbus commandos of Jabiim have proven that it's possible to become expert at bootbobbing. Corgolath makes some boots that will take you as high as 150 meters for about 550 credits. Double that if you're a quadruped.

Repulsorboots with inset coils, for low altitudes only

Parawings: Ages ago in the garbage pits of Coruscant, illegal racers figured out how to make personal flyers out of scavenged airfoils and low-power repulsorlifts. I'm not surprised it took Imperial Intelligence so long to copy the idea, but to be fair, their design is slightly less likely to kill you. This contraption is a pair of folding wings and an integrated repulsorlift engine attached to a harness, which you steer with your body movements. They say it's rated for an altitude of 5k but I wouldn't recommend it for anything other than reconnoitering or emergency escape. Cost? It's military, so you can't afford it. See your Guild contractor if you want to plead your case for renting one of ours.

Parawings are still experimental. Don't ask for them if you can't handle them.

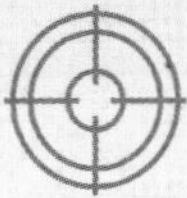

ADVANTAGES OF GUILD MEMBERSHIP

BY RATAK RAAM'LUK, ADMINISTRATIVE/PERSONNEL OFFICER, BOUNTY HUNTERS GUILD COUNCIL

There's nothing wrong with being an independent hunter. Really. If you enjoy digging up information about recently posted bounties, chasing down receivers to collect the bounties, counting your credits while watching your back, sorting out your finances to maintain your weapons and ship, and planning your retirement while you *occasionally* pursue acquisitions—whenever you have the chance—then by all means keep doing what you're doing.

In case your head is so thick that you missed the point: most independent hunters have so much to do that they spend the bulk of their time *not* hunting. Sure, some independents will tell you how much they save by not paying annual guild fees or sharing percentages of bounties, but instead of listening to those hunters, take a good look at what they have to show for their time and effort. Do you see aching joints and bad backs? Scarred flesh and third-rate prosthetics? Antiquated weapons and late-model starships that are one jump away from the junk heap? Honestly, do you want to wind up like that too?

This might surprise you, but the Guild isn't in business just to profit from capturing criminals. The Guild's primary function is to support Guild members in every aspect of their work. If you're not spending most of your time bagging acquisitions, you're losing money. Still think being an independent hunter is the way to go? Suit yourself. But if you're *smart*, you'll become a member of the Bounty Hunters Guild.

Want to know about the specific advantages of Guild membership? Read on and learn something.

EQUIPMENT

The Bounty Hunters Guild offers equipment and supplies to all members. Equipment includes everything from the essentials for operating in unique atmospheres and planetary environments to Guild-owned starships and privately subsidized transportation. Because the benefits derived from a successful hunt generally outweigh the cost of doing business, most equipment is supplied free of charge. If you require expensive or specialized items for a hunt, the Guild rents equipment at a fixed rate, the cost of which can be deducted from future bounties.

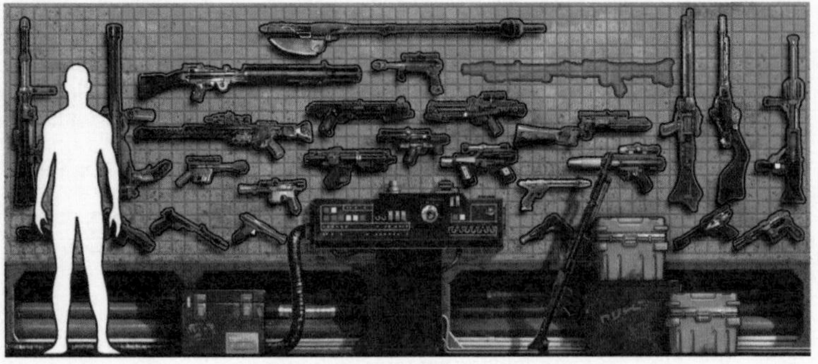

Guild armorers can supply the right weapons for any job.

INFORMATION

The Guild is much more than just a "bounty broker." It's a full-service information supplier. When you as a Guild member receive an assignment to pursue an acquisition, the Guild wants to make sure you'll have the most accurate data available. You'll receive frequent updates on current bounties, additional details regarding a subject's methods of operation, personal habits, known aliases and associates, and last known whereabouts. This service is also extended to affiliate guilds that allow freelance hunting, giving hunters an even greater edge as they pursue their own acquisitions.

MEDIATION

I'll let you know when I start caring about outraged civilians.
- Bossk

Let's say you're on a remote world, and an outraged civilian tells you that you exceeded your authority when you captured or killed an acquisition. Before you can respond, another local insists he's entitled to a share of the bounty because he directed you to the cantina where you found the acquisition. Then out pops the receiver, a bureaucrat who decides to withhold payment on a technicality. Let's also say that all three loudmouths are connected to some powerful people, so it would be a horrendous mistake to resolve this dispute with your blasters. Much as you'd love to riddle these guys with energy bolts, you might wind up in pieces, and you *definitely* won't get the bounty. Is that really how you want to live?

If you're a lone, independent hunter in this situation, you are truly on your own, pal. But if you belong to the Guild, which has officers prepared to act as your intermediaries and legal representatives, and thousands of other hunters itching to come crashing down on any meddlesome bores who stand between you and the bounty, you can bet your last credit that those troublemakers will think twice before wasting your time.

RECIPROCITY

The Bounty Hunters Guild and its affiliates have strong ties with law-enforcement institutions on many worlds, and these organizations maintain various reciprocity agreements. What does that mean to Guild members? If you venture into another syndicate's territory, you may apply for and expect to receive assistance from the local syndicate. The costs of such assistance are paid by the Guild and are deducted (with interest) from any forthcoming bounties. Be sure to itemize all expenses and pay your dues, and everyone will get along just fine.

REPAIRS

Did you lose a sensor array during a chase through an asteroid belt? Bust your blaster rifle over a fleeing felon's skull? Dent your landspeeder while ramming an acquisition into a wall? No worries if you're a Guild member. That's because any damage to Guild or personal property, from blasters to starships, can usually be repaired at little or no cost. Most repairs are done either at spaceports or at docking yards run by Guild members. If a Guild-owned facility isn't convenient, nearly any local weapons shop or shipping guild will be glad to make repairs for a tradeoff of services. Arrangements can also be made for local or planetary governments to extend repair services for a small fee. The Guild will take care of you and your stuff, allowing you to concentrate on getting those acquisitions.

-redit
here it's
ue: Guild
echanics
'd a great
b on my
umpMaster
5000.
- Dengar

REPUTATION

Why does the Empire enlist the Bounty Hunters Guild to pursue acquisitions, and keep coming back to the Guild for more? Because we're so

The Guild's strong commitment to publicity ensures our hunters are respected throughout the galaxy.

good-looking? No, it's because of our reputation. As a Guild member, you're part of that reputation.

Unlike most independents, the Guild has a promotional budget. We enjoy letting the galaxy know about our professionalism and the accomplishments of our members, as such publicity helps make the Guild more acceptable to the general public. Our most successful members garner special rates for especially delicate or dangerous hunts, and that should encourage you to do your best on behalf of the Guild, too.

The next time the Empire draws up a particularly lucrative bounty, trust they won't give the contract to just any law-enforcement agency. They'll give it to the Guild, because our reputation deserves it.

RETIREMENT

The word makes me want to kill everything in blaster range
- Bossk

Most hunters don't begin their careers planning for their retirement. That's their own fault. As for you, if you think the best way to die is in a blaze of glory, why don't you just walk into an ambush right now and get it over with? If you're lucky, maybe you'll survive the ambush and wind up dying in a poorhouse with other losers.

Yes, bounty hunting is a trade with a high fatality rate. However, the Guild has a proven track record of training and supporting hunters who want to survive to retirement age, which generally occurs much earlier than in other professions. The Guild believes loyal hunters should be rewarded for their years of service, which is why we offer a generous benefits package that allows you to live well long after you've delivered your last acquisition.

What if your skills remain sharp and you're not ready to hang up your blasters? The Guild also offers lucrative instructor contracts and insights to those willing and able to train younger hunters. As you impart your wisdom to a new generation of Guild members, you can bet your "retirement" is hardly the end, but rather the beginning of a new and highly valued career.

SANCTUARY

In the event that a Guild member runs afoul of a spaceport official or member of another syndicate, the Guild can offer sanctuary and will also defend the hunter against questionable charges. And when it comes to accountability and dealing with interplanetary governments and other law-enforcement agencies, Guild members have a big advantage over average citizens. That's because the Empire recognizes the necessity of bounty hunters, and grants the Guild a certain degree of autonomy in how we govern our members.

But be advised that the Guild has its own internal system of justice and punishment, and most galactic laws apply to Guild members, including laws established by the Empire. If you assault an Imperial officer or refuse to accept a direct order from a planetary governor, you might as well forget about seeking sanctuary from the Guild. If you believe you have a legitimate gripe with any Imperials, take it up with a Guild mediator. Imperial officials have the right to observe Guild criminal proceedings to ensure that Guild justice serves the best interest of the Empire. Is that fair? Don't ask me. All I know is, if it weren't for the Empire, we'd probably all be enslaved by Jedi by now.

In short, the Guild can't protect you from everyone and everything. You are responsible for your actions. But if you have need for judicial assistance, or require a safe house to maintain peace, the Guild won't let you down.

Good point! – Greedo

TRAINING

It has already been noted that retired hunters may become teachers to train Guild members, but that training is not limited to younger members. Even veteran hunters—the smart ones—are keen on improving their skills, learning new techniques, and testing new weapons. The Guild offers training for all members and encourages members to take full advantage of training resources.

Following the example of Trandoshan and Rodian hunters who maintain ancient hunting reserves in their own star systems, the Guild's resources include training facilities on numerous worlds. These facilities are staffed by instructors with extensive experience in everything from tracking and camouflage to marksmanship and demolitions. By special arrangement with Imperial authorities, the Guild also has almost unlimited access to train on three properties formerly used as Jedi chapter houses, the locations of which are a closely guarded secret, known only to Guild members and a select faction of Imperial officers.

KAMPARAS, BOGDEN & TELOS

BOBA

Guild trainers are usually ex-military.

EMPLOYMENT OPPORTUNITIES

BY 2T-DS, PERSONAL ASSISTANT TO THE ASSOCIATE MANAGING DIRECTOR OF ACCOUNTS

In case you're wondering, yes, I'm a droid, but I'm also a licensed Guild hunter. I've secured bounties for 209 criminal meatbags, and was listed among the top 10 money-earners for the Guild for three consecutive years before I joined the administrative team. I won't bother asking what *you've* done lately.

He could snag a million bounties and I'd sti hate droi - Bossk

Although you are obligated to accept and carry out any and every operation that your Guild contractor assigns, that's no excuse for you to sit around waiting for a bounty to fall in your lap. As long as you remember that the Guild is entitled to a percentage of any bounty you bring in, there's nothing stopping you from finding other hunting opportunities to enhance your reputation and accrue money.

My intention is to show you not only how to procure potential clients, but also what you need to know about clients' various financial and legal concerns pertaining to the posting of bounties. The money and the law are your concerns too, so make it your business to know them.

INFORMATION SERVICES

To obtain information that will help you perform your job, you have two prime options: the Imperial Enforcement DataCore and posting agencies. Both provide data that have been checked and approved by numerous planetary and Imperial authorities, but each has certain advantages.

In this section, you'll learn about various sources of information. Your professional associates are hardly your only sources. From the nearest spaceport to the most remote planetary stations, you'll find those who talk too much (with and without your persuasion). Take advantage of them, and listen well, because you never know where a good lead might come from.

Potential sources of information:

- Starpilots
- Technicians
- Mechanics
- Bartenders
- Service droids
- Miscellaneous individuals on the fringes of law-abiding society

If the Cantina janitor doesn't start delivering o the leads, I'm not giving him any more money.
— Greedo

IMPERIAL ENFORCEMENT DATACORE

The Imperial Office of Criminal Investigations (IOCI) serves as a central government for hunters. Almost every Imperial world has IOCI offices or at least one station, where hunters can purchase an Imperial Peace-Keeping Certificate (IPKC) license and any necessary permits, as well as deliver acquisitions. Each world has its own "board" for the Imperial Enforcement DataCore, a galaxy-wide information net that serves as the Empire's official listing of all legal, registered bounties. On more remote worlds, the DataCore can also be accessed through the offices of Imperial Enforcement, local law enforcement, licensing and registration agencies, public communications and message stations, and other government organizations and municipal outlets.

As a Guild member, you have access to the DataCore. Be advised: DataCore board data differ from one world to the next. Every board lists most-wanted and galaxy-wide postings, but the remaining listings are for local bounties pertinent to the given planet, as well as general bounties in that planet's system, sector, and region. In other words, don't expect to access the entire DataCore from a single board. If the IOCI listed every current bounty in the galaxy on a single board, hunters would waste time sifting through too much data about distant bounties.

The DataCore's primary menu lists only the name of the acquisition and the amount of the bounty. If you want specifics about criminal charges against the acquisition, the identity of the bounty's originator, or the location of the receiver, you'll have to pay for it. The IOCI offices currently charge hunters an average of 13.5 credits per hour for DataCore access and 5 credits for hunters to retrieve an entire bounty posting.

If you're tracking a criminal who's the subject of a legal bounty, but the criminal is in some area of the galaxy where the bounty isn't listed on the local DataCore boards, you'll need to provide proof of the bounty to the local IOCI office and request a Target Permit for the acquisition. You can obtain that proof from an IOCI office with a board that *does* list the bounty, and unless you have planned ahead that means you will have to backtrack to that office. IOCI-approved proof of a bounty comes in the form of an encrypted datacard that costs 10 credits. The Target Permit costs extra.

Obtain a proof of bounty if you want to get paid.

If you need to find other listings for a particular criminal, local IOCI offices can search boards on other planets, regardless of region or sector, for any listings of the criminal. For each planet's board they search, the IOCI charges a current average of 50 credits. However, if that furnishes the proof you require to capture a valuable acquisition, the charge incurred will be easily outweighed by the bounty.

POSTING AGENCIES

Except on worlds where bounty hunting is outlawed, you'll find at least one posting agency in just about any spaceport or major city. Posting agencies provide all the services of a local IOCI office and commonly act as "go-betweens" to facilitate the posting of bounties by corporations and private citizens within the Empire. Posting agencies are not directly affiliated with a specific guild or government organization, and they specialize in providing accurate, up-to-date information regarding the status of bounties.

In part, the agencies get this information directly from the Imperial Office of Criminal Investigations, which charges an annual fee to the agencies for access to the Imperial Enforcement DataCore. But to attract you as a customer, most agencies try to provide information on more bounties than the local DataCore board by maintaining links with DataCore boards on worlds in surrounding sectors.

A good posting agency doesn't rely on Imperial sources alone. It actively tracks criminals and trades data with other agencies and informants. Consequently, posting agencies have not only many bounty listings, but also more data about acquisitions than the DataCore. These data include extensive biographic information, reported sightings, and other facts related to the acquisition.

As noted above, you can expect to pay 10–15 credits per hour for DataCore access at an IOCI office. To access the DataCore from a posting agency, you will pay no more than 25 credits *per day*, a not inconsiderable savings if you anticipate reviewing the board for several hours. The Imperials claim that all Imperial bounties are posted on the DataCore first, before distribution to the posting agencies, and every hunter knows the advantage of getting information first. However, given professional expenses and the number of Imperial bounties at any given time, many hunters recognize the advantages of working with posting agencies.

You should visit posting agencies and become familiar with their employees. The agencies provide information to hunters and can also recommend experienced hunters to bounty originators and other potential clients. Although all posting agencies require originators to present clear evidence of wrongdoing before issuing a bounty, be aware that some agencies are less reputable than others, and will accept bounties with relatively flimsy evidence. Fortunately, the Empire verifies all evidence a posting agency claims to have seen.

FOR A PRICE, MOST IMPERIALS WILL VERIFY ANYTHING YOU PUT IN FRONT OF THEM.

BOBA

The Tanallay Surge posting agency, Tynna

Some posting agencies are authorized to issue permits and Imperial Peace-Keeping Certificate licenses. Because Imperial administrators often give posting agencies discounts to reduce datawork, posting agencies can offer large corporations modest savings on registration fees. Private citizens enjoy working with posting agencies to avoid dealing directly with the occasionally intimidating Imperial bureaucracy.

POSTING FEES

Many citizens question the prices for posting bounties. Given that a posting for a bounty to capture a murderer might contain the same amount of information as a post to capture a thief, citizens often ask, "Why does the posting for the murderer cost so much more?"

Some citizens just don't understand that posting a bounty isn't the same as posting a classified advertisement to sell a used landspeeder.

Posting fees for bounties vary wildly from one community or world to the next, as do permit requirements and registration fees. The biggest factors in determining posting fees are the amount of the bounty and how widely the posting will be distributed.

Approximate posting fees for different distribution areas:
Single continent or municipality: 10–100 credits
Planet- or system-wide: 50–500 credits
Sector-wide: 1,000–10,000 credits
Galaxy-wide: 50,000 credits

These figures are high to discourage citizens from issuing bounties for every petty offense and to cover all bounty-posting expenses for the duration of the bounty. If the public expects posting agencies to post bounties across large areas of the galaxy and to maintain operations and ensure the bounty remains active for as long as necessary, and if they expect bounty hunters to do a hazardous job on their behalf, they are required to pay for it.

INFORMATION BROKERS

Although the Bounty Hunters Guild boasts a strong department of information analysts, the Guild also relies on information brokers throughout the galaxy. Most are full-time brokers, but approximately 18 percent are merely occasional sellers of information. If all have anything in common, it's that they're excellent at getting answers without asking questions and at detecting anomalies and patterns in data.

While many privately employed information brokers prefer to remain anonymous, Kud'ar Mub'at is not one of them. Mub'at has been collating and providing data for the Bounty Hunters Guild for many years and is

One of the subsidiary starships operated by Kud'ar Mub'at, the Assembler

widely considered the best in his field. Mub'at also coordinates financial transactions between the Guild and thousands of law-enforcement agencies and bounty hunting–related associates, ensuring prompt payments for the bounties collected by Guild members. Your Guild contractor is your conduit to Mub'at, and you are advised not to contact him personally. He lives on a heavily armed spacecraft that discourages uninvited guests. (See "Contractor Resources," p. 39.) NOT ANYMORE. BOBA

NON-STANDARD IMPERIAL BOUNTIES

Aside from bounties posted by civil government authorities, bounties are also issued by military and intelligence authorities. The Imperial military relies on the DataCore to post and distribute bounties, which are generally offered against individuals wanted for high treason, under circumstances in which the military is incapable of bringing the criminals to justice. Be advised: whenever the bounty posting indicates an act of treason, the Imperial Security Bureau (ISB) and its Enforcement Division will always be directly involved.

But not all military bounties wind up on the DataCore. When the Imperials want to bring in an individual for questioning, possibly because the individual possesses classified information, they offer "confidential bounties" to Guild hunters. The ISB's Enforcement Division oversees all such hunts, and usually has every reason to expect you'll conduct the hunt with extreme discretion. Such contracts pay better than ones you can actually talk about with fellow hunters. Bring in the acquisition quietly and keep your mouth shut, and you will not only score points with your contractor and the ISB, but you will probably find yourself lined up with more such work. You might even wind up on the ISB's short list of hunters qualified for "special assignments."

If you don't know what an ISB special assignment is, it's because you're not yet ready for one. If ISB special assignments were real, I'd know about them. - Bossk

PRIVATE POSTINGS

While the Empire represents the primary source of bounties in the galaxy, other sources include corporations, private groups, and wealthy patrons. Bounties for such alternative sources are generally referred to as "private postings." Private postings must be registered through the Imperial Office of Criminal Investigations (IOCI) and must meet strict conditions.

Requirements for private postings:

- Verifiable proof of wrongdoing is submitted
- The face value of the bounty is paid in advance
- The bounty's originator or the originator's representative pays the required IOCI registration fee.

Private citizens and companies post bounties because their local officials or law-enforcement agencies lack the personnel or inclination to bring wanted criminals to justice. You'll get the same story from larger corporations, which tend to issue bounties for crimes involving criminal trespass, property damage, assault on corporate personnel, theft of sensitive data, and any other infraction related to the disruption of trade. If you want to know the real reason why citizens and companies choose to contact the Guild, you need only watch the HoloNet news for yet another report about corrupt officials refusing to prosecute crimes ranging from theft to murder. There are innumerable documented cases of disreputable law officers and bureaucratic bunglers, so it's no wonder more and more people rely upon the Guild for their peacekeeping needs.

EXPEDITORS

Because Guild administrators and contractors provide a buffer between Guild hunters and the Imperial bureaucracy, you may think you don't need to stay abreast of new postings, local planetary regulations, and hunt restrictions. Incorrect. Just because you're contractually obligated to accept assignments from your Guild contractor doesn't suggest you should embrace ignorance. Now the droid is calling us ignorant? - Bossk

Granted, your Guild contractor *will* take care of you, but the more you know about the business, the better. Especially if you're interested in taking on freelance assignments. Unless you're confident that you can manage your own financial resources, invest profits, make necessary payoffs, promote your reputation, interact with posting agencies and corporations to secure lucrative employment opportunities, and keep yourself apprised of every newly authorized Imperial bounty worth your consideration, you'll need professional help. Specifically, you'll need an expeditor.

Expeditors typically act as intermediaries between bounty hunters and Imperials, and manage nearly every aspect of business for hunters. Usually headquartered in sector capitals or a planet's largest city, expeditors are experts at obtaining the maximum number of bounty-related credits for themselves and their clients. With a licensed and bonded expeditor, you won't have to worry about whether you have the proper permits to operate in any given sector. Expeditors allow you to focus on the hunt.

For their services, expeditors typically charge a flat fee (3–5 percent of any bounties or contracts arranged through their offices). Whether you're an independent hunter or a Guild member operating in unfamiliar territory, good expeditors will earn their keep by keeping you out of trouble.

RECEIVERS

When you capture your acquisition, remember that your job isn't done until you obtain payment. As previously noted, the receiver is the being, location, or entity to which an acquisition can be delivered. Only upon delivery are you entitled to receive the full bounty.

Depending on the terms of the bounty, you can choose to deliver live acquisitions or their identifiable remains directly to the receiver or to any Imperial law enforcement office on any planet. If you choose an Imperial office, the Empire will charge transportation and guard fees for delivering the acquisition to the receiver. Although Guild administrators acknowledge that certain extenuating circumstances may necessitate leaving an acquisition with Imperial authorities, such as when a hunter is compelled to deliver one acquisition in order to pursue another, this is rarely profitable for the hunter or the Guild. Imperial transportation fees vary depending on the number of armed guards required, travel time and distance to the receiver, and any special requirements the acquisition may demand.

Make sure the acquisition is secure before handing off to a receiver.

Breakdown of fees charged by the Empire to transport and guard acquisitions:

Transport within a system: 100–1,000 credits
Transport within a sector: 500–5,000 credits
Transport within a region: 20,000 credits minimum
Transport across the galaxy: 50,000 credits minimum

Imperial officials also typically withhold payment of the bounty until after the acquisition has been delivered to the receiver. Therefore, you'll either have to return to an Imperial office for payment or wait for payment to be forwarded to you, your Guild contractor, or an expeditor. If all that isn't enough to convince you that it's more economical to personally deliver the acquisition to the receiver, you should also know that if the acquisition escapes or accidentally dies while in Imperial custody, the Empire is *not* responsible. Not to dismiss the option of entrusting the highly competent Empire with delivering acquisitions to receivers, but a more cost-effective alternative is to arrange transportation—preferably a well-armed corvette—through your Guild contractor or private party.

NEVER
CIDENTALLY
WITH THE
EMPIRE.
BOBA

Book transportation aboard a secure starship if you've got hot merchandise.

Whether the receiver is the bounty's originator, a law-enforcement agent, or a detention facility, be advised that every receiver may be a repeat customer, and that you are a member and representative of the Bounty Hunters Guild. You are expected to be courteous to all receivers and to give them no reason to question your professionalism. If you successfully deliver the acquisition but the receiver reneges on paying the bounty, do not argue. Simply inform the receiver that if they choose to break their contract, a task force of Guild administrators will meet with them to resolve the matter immediately.

Imperial detention centers don't like hunters, so don't overstay your welcome.

CORPORATE TERRITORIES

Numerous corporations own vast territories throughout the galaxy, from continents on planets and the worlds themselves to entire sectors. Although the Empire has jurisdiction in such territories, the owning corporations have as much authority over the residents and "employees"—*not citizens*—as the companies deem necessary. The owning corporations are essentially local governments, left to police themselves, with the provision that they supply sufficient tax revenues to the Empire. Corporations do not take kindly to thieves and unscrupulous business

Look into money-making opportunities in the Corporate Sector. — Greedo

operators, and they are entitled to post bounties on wanted beings within their company territory. They also tend to pay extremely well. It stands to reason that this is of interest to the Bounty Hunters Guild.

The Guild has extensive experience in working on behalf of large corporations, and it trains Guild hunters to navigate the legal, logistical, and economic challenges unique to corporate territories. The largest corporate territory in the galaxy is the Corporate Sector, which includes over 30,000 habitable star systems, and is owned and governed by the Corporate Sector Authority. You can expect to pay as you enter the Corporate Sector and as you exit. But because there is still potential for you and the Guild to make a considerable profit, the Corporate Sector can be well worth the price of admission, as well as the exit toll.

Be advised: additional fees *will* be levied. Corporations have the authority to charge hunters for permit and capture fees, not to mention fees for temporary insurance while traveling specific routes. Once you enter a corporate territory, you will be subject to the corporation's laws and specific contract provisions, so the most important thing to keep in mind is the corporation's boundaries. If you pursue an acquisition out of the corporate zone, and the acquisition is not wanted in the Empire, you will be violating various laws, and subject to criminal charges and substantial fines. Corporate zones take a dim view of anyone who bypasses their judicial systems, as they expect to profit from extraditions to foreign territories.

If the Guild receives a posting for an acquisition wanted in Imperial space, but who has escaped into the Corporate Sector, your Guild contractor can give you detailed instructions, but trust that the Corporate Sector *is* subject to certain Imperial laws, and that the no amount of money can buy immunity from Imperial prosecution. If for any reason your Guild contractor is unavailable to advise you about pursuit into the Corporate Sector, you should seek professional assistance from a licensed expeditor familiar with the territory's laws, fees, and permit requirements.

Corporate zones aren't for hunters. They're for bean counters. — Dengar

THE HUTT KAJIDICS

Older than the Old Republic are the legendarily capitalistic Hutt *kajidics*, a loose term referring to Hutt clans and business enterprises, but which can be translated as, "Somebody's got to have it, why not us?" The Hutts rule directly over a number of worlds in the region classified as Hutt Space, but they operate throughout the galaxy. Their wide range of business interests includes everything from the interstellar trade of exotic goods to managing sports arenas and spaceports.

The Hutt kajidics employ members of all species and are willing to hire anyone who can bring them more money or facilitate their constant pursuit of pleasure. "Anyone" definitely includes bounty hunters, as Hutts spare no expense in chasing down those who cheat or betray them. Although Hutts rely upon the Bounty Hunters Guild on a case-by-case basis, some have been known to arrange long-term contracts for Guild hunters to remain with or close to the Hutts, so that the hunters are more accessible.

Hutts nurse plenty of grudges and hire plenty of hunters.

AFFILIATE BOUNTY HUNTER GUILDS

BY VA GOBOLUNGNUM,

BOUNTY HUNTERS GUILD BRANCH COORDINATOR

Since the foundation of the Bounty Hunters Guild, and especially since the foundation of the Empire, a number of affiliate bounty hunter guilds have sprung up throughout the galaxy. Also known as syndicates, these subguilds are privately owned organizations that hire bounty hunters, deduct a percentage of bounty revenues to support the organization, and are involved with training and supporting hunters. These syndicates were founded to better enforce bounties within specific sectors, and some syndicates are more exclusive than others, but make no mistake about who's in charge. The Bounty Hunters Guild oversees *all* the syndicates listed in this section.

AND THE EMPIRE OVERSEES THE BHG.

BOBA

The syndicates include numerous chapter houses. Many of the older chapter houses were originally established in remote sectors so the Guild could simultaneously manage such areas and also prevent competition from unethical independent hunters. The major chapters are distinguished by specialized services and a limited range of operations, and each has various differences involving the respective corporate governing structures, membership and training opportunities, and payment schedules. If you're interested in joining a Guild chapter house, or are considering transferring from one chapter house to another, you should examine this section damned carefully.

The following pages present detailed information about notable hunter chapter houses and syndicates currently operating within the Empire. There are many other famous and influential guilds in the Empire, but the ones included here are a representative cross-section of the state of guilds in the galaxy. To better comprehend the unique characteristics of each house, please consult the following key:

Organization: The name of the hunter institution

Administrator: The chief executive officer, owner, or controlling faction

Size: Approximate size of the institution, expressed in terms of active hunters and support personnel

Contract Specialization: The type of bounties that are the house's specialty, if applicable

Influence: A relative measure of the institution's political and financial clout within the Empire, and the institution's ability to influence Imperial policy (measured as marginal, nominal, moderate, substantial)

Sphere of Operations: Relative scope of the institution's activities

Headquarters: Location of the guild home offices

Membership: Means by which individual membership is granted

Dues: Individual membership dues, where applicable

Gap: Administration points applied to a hunter's bounty where applicable, deducted as a percentage from any bounties claimed by the hunter

HOUSE BENELEX

Organization: House Benelex Bounty Hunters Guild

Administrator: Corvastan Benelex

Size: 1,279 hunters; 7,600 administrative and support personnel

Contract Specialization: Kidnapping retrievals, LAACDocs (to 10,000 credits)

Influence: Moderate

Sphere of Operations: Current operations throughout the Outer Rim Territories, selected Outer Expansion Region sectors (Fellwe, Ehosiq, Lostar), the Corporate Sector

Headquarters: Paqualis III

Membership: Sponsorship by one other member

Dues: 700 credits (annual)

Gap: 3%

Founded by former bounty hunter Corvastan Benelex, House Benelex exists as a corporate offspring of the Drearian Defense Conglomerate (DDC), manufacturers of specialized weapons.

House Benelex formed after Corvastan Benelex rescued the son of DDC president Mardu Avoa from Thalassian slavers. During the rescue, Benelex executed the slavers' ringleader but suffered a debilitating blaster wound that effectively ended his career as a hunter. While recuperating in a DDC medical facility, Benelex gave serious consideration to his future and how he might turn his loss into an advantage. Benelex met with DDC vice-president Shiko Tanderris, and requested a loan of two million credits, along with certain arms concessions that would enable him to establish a Guild house specializing in the retrieval of kidnapping victims and other hostages. With the tacit agreement that DDC's marketing department would have creative input on promotion for the house, Tanderris readily granted the loan, and House Benelex was born.

From the start, House Benelex attracted not only bounty hunters who saw something noble in dedicating their skills to rescuing hostages, but also many specialists in counterterrorism and hostage negotiation. Now in its second decade of operation, House Benelex has successfully carried out numerous rescue missions, including several highly publicized rescues in the Chalenor System. House Benelex has also profited by taking advantage of certain Imperial programs, such as issuing Legal Authorization for Advanced Confinement Documents

Rumor has it some Benelex hunters were staging kidnappings so they could "rescue" the victims and collect the payouts. – Dengar

THE RUMORS WERE TRUE. CORVASTAN BENELEX CONTRACTED ME TO FIX THE PROBLEM. BOBA

(LAACDocs) to track down acquisitions. House Benelex is widely regarded as the perfect blend of entrepreneurial ingenuity and corporate sponsorship in the industry of bounty hunting.

Corvastan Benelex versus the Thalassians. This image hangs in every Benelex guildhouse.

HOUSE TRESARIO

Organization: House Tresario Bounty Hunters Guild

Administrator: Rovan Tresario

Size: 1,767 hunters; 9,659 administrative and support personnel

Contract Specialization: No bounties under 15,000 credits

Influence: Moderate

Sphere of Operations: Throughout the Empire; 22% of operations in Core or surrounding regions

Headquarters: Baradas II

Membership: Sponsorship by at least two other members

Dues: 1,000 credits (annual)

Gap: 8%

House Tresario was founded by former Imperial Navy officers led by Rovan Tresario, and it maintains strong ties to the Imperial military. This syndicate is headquartered in the Colonies Region and specializes in hunting pirates.

As a Navy officer, Rovan Tresario's career was marked by continued frustration at the hands of pirates, notably the notorious "Scourge of the Seven Sectors," Reginald Barkbone. After retiring from the Navy, Tresario joined with fellow retired officers who, like him, had been vexed by pirates, and felt compelled to resume their war against piracy. Pooling their resources, they managed to hire several bounty hunters and sent them after various elusive pirate leaders in the Colonies Region.

Although efforts to apprehend Reginald Barkbone have so far been unsuccessful, Tresario's group not only avenged their military careers, but also profited from the bounties on many pirates. Soon after founding House Tresario, they began expanding their operations to other regions, and have been going after bigger and bigger Imperial contracts with each passing year

Rovan Tresario

THE SLAVER SYNDICATE

Organization: The Zygerian Slaver Syndicate

Administrator: Zygerian Clan Pr'ollerg

Size: Unknown, but believed to be over 2,000 active hunters and slavers

Contract Specialization: Bounties with slaving rights

Influence: Nominal

Sphere of Operations: Isolated regions of the Outer Rim Territories

Headquarters: Karazak

Membership: Private initiation fee (believed to cost between 2,000 and 5,000 credits, sometimes waived for those with relatives in the organization)

Dues: None

Gap: None

Under the ineffectual laws of the hypocritical Old Republic, the business of slavery was long illegal but nevertheless practiced in the Outer Rim Territories. All that changed with Imperial Decree A-SL-4557.607.232, which wisely expedited and streamlined laws for buying, selling, trafficking, and owning slaves. A number of slaver cooperatives are currently operating in the Outer Rim, but the best known is the Slaver Syndicate.

A loose confederation of bounty hunters, the Slaver Syndicate is controlled by the Zygerian Clan Pr'ollerg. It dictates which bounties to hunt, how much to pay for slaving rights, and when and where to act. The Syndicate generally pursues modest bounties, mostly acquisitions guilty of minor infractions. Such individual acquisitions are typically overlooked or dismissed by more experienced hunters because they aren't profitable, but what the syndicate loses in per capita bounty collections they make up for in sheer volume.

Furthermore, live captures are usually brought to systems with liberal slaving laws, where they are purchased and resold as slaves.

The slave types most heavily trafficked by the Slaver Syndicate include native Mandalorians and the Twi'lek. The Syndicate occasionally deals in the transport of Wookiees, but not to any great extent, as the Trandoshans have a near monopoly on the market for Wookiees.

HOUSE PARAMEXOR

Organization: Paramexor Guild of Hunters

Administrator: Guild Master Janq Paramexor

Size: 623 hunters; 1,740 administrative and support personnel

Contract Specialization: Only bounties involving murder or attempted murder accepted

Influence: Moderate, but increasing

Sphere of Operations: Galactic Core and surrounding regions; some operations lead to outlying regions, but no permanent offices are maintained

Headquarters: Denevar

Membership: Sponsorship by three other members

Dues: 300 credits (annual)

Gap: 3%

Founded by Janq Paramexor and headquartered on the planet Denevar, House Paramexor is dedicated to the elimination of those who deliberately kill their fellow creatures for sport or profit, and is distinguished by accepting bounties in which the acquisition is wanted dead, for crimes related to murder or attempted murder. Paramexor's hunters have a well-deserved reputation of being consummate professionals, and are also fiercely loyal to their Guild Master.

Janq Paramexor

Janq Paramexor was formerly a military officer who survived a duel that resulted in internal injuries that left him paralyzed from the waist down. Confined to a mobile life-support pod for over a quarter of a century, Paramexor developed a deep appreciation for all life forms, and a corresponding abhorrence for those who take lives without just cause. Several like-minded patrons helped

Paramexor's life-support pod is loaded with concealed weapons.
— Dengar

Paramexor found his organization and continue to support his cause.

Paramexor provides his hunters with the best health and personal services, luxurious accommodations, and generous retirement plans. Paramexor deliberately keeps his total number of hunters to under 1,000, and shows little inclination to expand his operations to other specialties.

HOUSE NEUVALIS

Organization: House Neuvalis Bounty Hunters Guild

Administrators: Marjan and Feras Neuvalis

Size: 6,790 hunters; 66,740 administrative and support personnel

Contract Specialization: No bounties under 20,000 credits

Influence: Substantial

Sphere of Operations: Throughout the Empire; 20% of operations in or near Galactic Core

Headquarters: Plexis

Membership: Sponsorship by one other member; survival of initiation test

Dues: 500 credits (annual)

Gap: 10%

NEUVALIS—POSSIBLE TIES W/ REBELS. INVESTIGATE
BOBA

One of the youngest Guild houses in operation, House Neuvalis is also one of the most fiscally solvent. House Neuvalis has a strict policy of accepting only the most profitable Imperial and Corporate contracts, and refusing to contract any bounties under 20,000 credits. This policy attracts wealthy clients as well as highly skilled representatives. If any Neuvalis guild hunter is unable to fulfill a selected contract within one year, the guild will pay the originator double the face value of the bounty. Because House Neuvalis is not in the business of losing money, this policy encourages clients' confidence and motivates Guild hunters to collect acquisitions as soon as possible. The posting of bonds in advance has the net result of both the Empire and private sector sources coming repeatedly to Neuvalis with their most important bounties.

RAGNAR SYNDICATE

Organization: Ragnar Bounty Hunter Syndicate

Administrator: Reshton Severindas

Size: 270 active hunters; 4,535 reserve hunters; 2,700 administrative and support personnel

Contract Specialization: Paramilitary special operations

Influence: Moderate, but increasing

Sphere of Operations: Outer Rim Territories, expanding to other areas

Headquarters: Ragnar VIII

Membership: Personal selection by House CEO

Dues: None, but new members pay higher gaps for their first three years

Gap: 20% (new members); 3% (bounties below 5,000 credits), 4% (bounties above 5,000 credits)

The Ragnar Syndicate is unusual in that it hires its hunters on a contract-by-contract basis, which minimizes overhead costs, and allows its hunters to engage in extensive freelance assignments. Hunters can be recalled from syndicate standby lists for special missions as needed. While most of the syndicate's revenue is generated from the collection of Imperial bounties, the syndicate's employees are known to engage in anti-terrorism, sabotage, and assassination.

The syndicate hires out its hunters for special missions that are quasi-military in nature and routinely matches experienced and novice hunters on missions. This arrangement allows novices to receive training with a greater degree of safety and to provide assistance to their trainers.

Reshton Severindas

HOUSE RENLISS

Organization: House Renliss Bounty Hunters Guild

Administrators: Jalindas and Gratina Renliss

Size: 244 active huntresses; 1,249 administrative and support personnel

Contract Specialization: Bounties issued against males

Influence: Marginal, but increasing

Sphere of Operations: Active operations in the Galactic Core, Core Worlds, the Colonies, the Inner Rim Planets, Hutt Space, the Corporate Sector, and also selected territories in the Outer Expansion Zone and Outer Rim Territories

Headquarters: Dartessex IV

Membership: Female hunters only; personal selection by House CEOs

Dues: Personal arrangement with House CEOs

Gap: 5%

Founded by sisters Jalindas and Gratina Renliss, House Renliss accepts only female hunters, and accepts bounties on male acquisitions only. According to a House Renliss promotional tract, each hunter receives a level of personalized training and attention unavailable in other guilds.

Although House Renliss has been in operation for several years, the organization's origins, as well as the backgrounds of its founders, remain a mystery to outsiders. Numerous reports, however, indicate Renliss has ties with members of the Imperial intelligence community, and that Renliss's profits have increased annually and substantially.

NO MYSTERY. RENLISS SISTERS FORMER MEMBERS OF IMPERIAL DEEP-COVER TEAM. IMPERIAL INTEL USES RENLISS TO GET RID OF SCUM IN THEIR OWN ORGANIZATION. BOBA

Jalindas and Gratina Renliss

MANTIS SYNDICATE

Organization: Mantis Bounty Hunter Syndicate

Administrator: Lady Marina Mantis

Size: 985 hunters; 845 combat support personnel; 220 administrative personnel

Contract Specialization: High-risk assignments, private retainer paramilitary operations up to battalion level

Influence: Substantial

Sphere of Operations: Current operations centered in and around Sarin sector, Outer Rim Territories

Headquarters: Santarine

Membership: Active recruitment by Lady Mantis, as well as selective reenlistment

Dues: 150 credits (annual), waived for enlisted hunters

Gap: 3-5% (sliding scale based on value of bounty and years of service for syndicate)

Owned and directed by Lady Marina Mantis of the Sarin Sector, the Mantis Syndicate consists of specialists drawn from bounty hunter backgrounds and is able to put large numbers of experienced troops—company- and battalion-sized units—in the field on short notice.

...are just mercenary gangsters. Beats me how they're Guild affiliates. — Dengar

Lady Marina Mantis and her mercenary-styled hunters

HOUSE SALAKTORI

Organization: House Salaktori Bounty Hunters Guild

Administrator: Jeslor Salaktori

Size: 2,240 hunters; 47,300 administrative and support personnel

Contract Specialization: Imperial bounties over 10,000; corporate and private bounties over 20,000

Influence: Substantial

Sphere of Operations: Throughout the Empire

Headquarters: Resht VII

Membership: Personal selection by House CEO

Dues: 1,000 credits (annual)

Gap: 4%

Let the Guild hereafter be unto you as your mother and father.
Let this house stand with you as a friend in need.
Let this home forever take pride in you as a lover who delights in your prowess.
Those who bore you may betray the Empire tomorrow.
He who in friendship stands by your side may slide the blade in all the easier.
She who shares your sleep may seek to strangle you in it.
After all forsake you, only your Guild shall remain to fortify and protect you.
Only your Guild understands exactly who and what you are, and dares to care about you just the same.

—From *The Foundation Creed*
Salaktori Hunter Guild

One of the oldest and most influential hunter guilds, the preeminent House Salaktori has maintained its leadership among the guilds for many generations. The guild is under the direction of Chief Executive Officer Jeslor Salaktori, who inherited his position from his father seventeen years ago. Membership is restricted to only the very best hunters, as judged by the CEO.

Never one to shy from a fight in either the field or the corporate arena, Jeslor Salaktori has personally defended his hunters against Imperial administrators

Who do I have to shoot to get invited to House Salaktori? – Greedo

Greedo couldn't even have shot himself if he'd tried.
– Bossk

Jeslor Salaktori

who have attempted to inhibit hunting operations. He continues to pressure Imperials to limit the restrictive practice of assessing "collateral damage" fines against hunters.

The unofficial motto of House Salaktori is "We take care of our own—one way or the other." A notorious HoloNet investigative report claimed Salaktori applies this motto in all aspects of business, including revenge, and presented data that implied no one responsible for the death of a Salaktori hunter has lived more than one year after the incident. An immediate and more carefully researched follow-up report revealed every one of the alleged "revenge deaths" had been ruled accidental.

NO ACCIDENTS. THE FIRST REPORT WAS RIGHT.
BOBA

t to
mire
laktori
or going
ose-to-
se with
mps.
Dengar

For you, my son, a glimpse into the minds of my enemies.
JANGO

FOR YOU, MY DAUGHTER. MA
YOU BEGIN TO UNDERSTAND.
BOBA

DEATH WATCH

BA'JURNE KYR'TSAD MANDO'AD

My name is Tor Vizsla. I am commander of the Death Watch, and the secret Mand'alor.
In darkness I don beskar'gam, so that one day the faithful may do so in daylight.
In secret I wield the Darksaber, so that one day our honor shall be apparent to all.
In silence I summon the worthy, so that one day our cause will ring out.

FOREWORD

You are reading this because you have been chosen as a Rally Master, charged with training recruits, preparing Watchers for operations and commanding them in battle. Like Cassus Fett's Rally Masters of ancient times, you must educate and inspire our warriors, so they understand their heritage and will sacrifice their lives for it.

What is that heritage? Here you will read the true history of our warriors, passed covertly from armored hand to armored hand, untainted by the lies of the so-called New Mandalorians, the Republic, or the Jedi sorcerers.

member, Boba:
e past is a trap
-Aurra

Here, too, you shall learn of our armor, weapons, strategies, and goals—information vital to our survival. For we are the Mando'ade—the Mandalorians. War is our birthright, and in war we measure ourselves against our forebears.

THE TRUE HISTORY OF THE MANDALORIANS

Our history begins with the Taung, the Shadow Warriors we honor as our Progenitors. They originally dwelled on Coruscant, but their enemies drove them into the Outer Rim. Their clans traveled from planet to planet on orders from their war chief, who interpreted the will of their now-extinct gods: Kad Ha'rangir, the all-seeing creator of tests and trials; Hod Ha'ran the trickster, agent of fickle fortune; and Arasuum the god of sloth, an enemy whispering and seducing with promises of peace. Many planets fell to the Progenitors' blades, and many civilizations quaked at the mere mention of their names.

The ancient Mandalorian deities were led by the all-seeing Kad Ha'rangir (left), shown here beside the trickster god Hod Ha'ran (center) and the slothful Arasuum (right).

Some seven millennia ago, the Shadow Warriors came to Mandalore and cleansed surrounding space of species unworthy and unclean—the Fenelar, Tlönians, and others. Here, in Mandalorian Space, they took the technologies of conquered species and reshaped them for warcraft. Here, amid Mandalore's lush forests and fields, their strength grew and their great purpose was revealed: a generations-long endeavor that would prepare the way for us.

We call the Shadow Warriors our Progenitors, though we do not share their blood, and their bodies were those of beasts, not humans. We do so because their leaders forged the Mando'ade into warrior bands and taught them to treasure family, clan, and honor. Their teachings became the Resol'nare, the Six Actions that make us Mandalorians: raising the young to seek honor and glory, wearing armor, defending one's self and one's family, supporting one's clan, speaking a common language, and owing fealty to the leader of the clans.

Betrayed by Jedi: What a surprise. -Aurra

Four millennia ago, the Progenitors began the Great Shadow Crusade, which others call the Great Sith War. Led by Mandalore the Indomitable, they attacked the central systems from which they had been driven. Ultimately they were betrayed by the Jedi and their Sith brethren, but from that day forward the name Mandalorian was feared by the Republic's decadent and useless idlers. Closer to home, the stage was set for the Emergence—the transformation of the clans into the modern Mando'ade.

Mandalore the Indomitable

Of the ancient Mandalores, we hold none in higher esteem than Mandalore the Ultimate, the Great Shadow Father of our clans. On Shogun, then as now the planet of visions, Mandalore the Ultimate received a staggering prophecy:

Think twice when someone gives you the opportunity to die. -Aurra

The age of the Taung was ending, but their great work was unfinished. To survive, the Mando'ade must be transformed.

It was a terrible burden, but Mandalore the Ultimate bore it with honor. He opened the clans to all who proved themselves in battle and followed the warrior codes. Non-Taung were no longer confined to vassalship, but could be full-fledged Mandalorian warriors. Our forefathers were among these new Mando'ade, and soon proved that they were ready to lead the clans.

These new warriors became known as the Neo-Crusaders, and their crucible was the Onslaught, remembered by the Republic as the Mandalorian Wars. The Onslaught would ultimately fail, turned back by the scheming of Republic machinesmiths and the sheer numbers of the dar'manda. Mandalore the Ultimate died on Malachor V, in the clash we know as Ani'la Akaan, the Great Last Battle. The clans were scattered and the Republic was triumphant.

Mandalorian Neo-Crusaders advancing under fire during the Onslaught

Ani'la Akaan was a dark day, but the Onslaught's purpose was never galactic conquest. Rather, it was meant to engineer the Emergence. In that respect, it succeeded: our forefathers became the new clan chiefs, chosen to continue the Progenitors' struggle. Within another generation, they would found a new line of Mandalores, and the days of the Shadow Warriors were ended.

The Progenitors are extinct, but we do not mourn them, for they fulfilled their destiny. While gone in flesh, in spirit they dwell within us still—the very

With successes like these, who needs failures? - Hondo

planes and angles of our helmets and visors recall their faces. We are their legacy, their vengeance on a galaxy that scorned and exiled them. This is why when we chant *Dha Werda Verda*, the first words are:

The ash of the Taung beats strong within the Mandalorians' hearts
We are the rage of the Warriors of the Shadow
The first noble sons of Mandalore.

The millennia since Ani'la Akaan have brought constant tests for the Mando'ade, with our enemies conspiring endlessly to destroy us. But fire strengthens beskar. Pain, defeat, and loss eliminate the weak and elevate the strong. Amid darkness and misery we have persevered, and our enemies' machinations have only sharpened our purpose and strengthened our resolve.

After Ani'la Akaan, weak Mandalores led the clans, and our honor ebbed—these were the years of the Arasuum, the Stagnation. Then, 11 centuries ago, with the galaxy plunged into darkness by war and disease, Mandalore the Uniter called the best and brightest Mandalorians home from the distant stars to which fate had cast them.

The Return strengthened Mandalore, which emerged as a rival of the Republic. Under the Uniter and the strong Mandalores who followed him, our homeworld became the protector of many star systems and the center of an honorable civilization. Warriors ruled, protecting the artisans, manufacturers, and laborers who supported them, and who were supported in turn by vassals and servants.

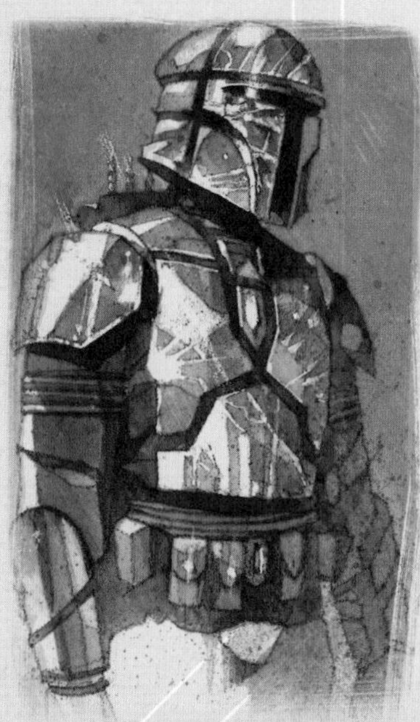
Mandalore the Uniter

A "perfect society" wouldn't be defeate[d] by Jedi. -Aurr[a]

This perfect society threatened the Republic. Seven centuries ago, their craven, hut'uune warships and Jedi bombarded our worlds. They incinerated Mandalore's farmland and forests, leaving much of our homeworld a forsaken desert of fine white sand, and then occupied our worlds. They killed, exiled, or disarmed our warriors and

Republic warships scour Mandalore during the Annihilation.

I wonder if Vizsla really wrote this. He was a thug. Sounds more like Priest, or Requ. Maybe the younger Vizsla. That one likes speeches. —JANGO

suppressed our ancient codes. The Republic called this dishonorable assault the Mandalorian Excision, as if we were cancerous tissue to be cut out of the galaxy. We call it the Dral'Han—the Annihilation.

The Annihilation birthed the evils we now fight against. To rule us, the Republic installed puppets who had sought a foolish peace with the Senators and their Jedi. In the centuries since the Annihilation, this line of Anti-Mandalores—leaders of the self-styled New Mandalorians—have forfeited our honor, buying us soft lives of sloth and dependence.

Bah! Sloth is one of my favorite things! - Hondo

Weary of war and deluded by lies, many of the Mando'ade accepted the Anti-Mandalores and the illegitimate rule of the Faithless, as we call the New Mandalorians. But others passed the old ways down in secret, teaching their children the Six Actions and keeping our history alive. These brave few became known as the Aka'liit, the Mandalorian Faithful. The division between the Faithful and the Faithless split every clan: members of the Ordos, Fetts, Kryzes, Awauds, Priests, Gedycs, and, yes, Vizslas belonged to both sides in our long struggle.

The Faithful forged a secret network of clan representatives. A generation after the Annihilation, this network appointed the first of a line of True Mandalores, to whom the Faithful secretly offered allegiance. This was the time of the ba'slan shev'la, the decision to disappear and wait for an opportune chance to strike back. Our warriors became known as the Alor'a Aka'liit—the Vanguard of the Faithful. *Only Mandos could turn failure into national epic. -Aurra*

Two centuries ago, we saw the corrupt Republic finally dying of old age. But tragically, the Faithful found themselves divided. This division began with a crusade against the Ithullans, whose machinations had become a threat. We seized their orbital stations, blacking out their communications and deactivating the power-beam arrays. Then we raided the darkened cloudtop cities, splitting their reactor bulbs like overripe Kalevalan quench-gourds. One by one they plunged into the fathomless Ithullan Depths, until Ithull was clean.

Clean and worthle
Revenge is bad business.
- Hondo

The Faithful hunt down Ithullan holdouts.

As always, the soft, sentimental Republic professed shock that others might take decisive action, and pretended to admire a weak and unworthy species. While we had expected that, we had never imagined that some among the Faithful would take their side, arguing that in upholding our honor we had damaged our cause. As though any worthy cause can exist without honor!

Honor is how the powerful convince the foolish to sacrifice themselves. -Aurra

Other disagreements soon followed. Some of the Faithful, the so-called True Mandalorians, wanted to dictate how all of us should earn credits for ourselves and our families, and they sought to supervise our conduct in a hostile galaxy. The wiser among us understood that in times of war it is only the ruthless—those who free themselves of the traps of pity and vacillation—who survive.

The breaking point came nearly three decades ago, when the Faithful made a terrible error, choosing Jaster Mereel as the True Mandalore. Mereel had been a lawman, a Journeyman Protector on Concord Dawn, until he murdered hese are LIES. Jaster sought true honor, ol the ight to nore laws r moral odes. zsla's ath Watch s nothing l a ense for urder. JANGO

a superior officer. Wracked by guilt, he concluded that the flaw lay not in his own heart but in the universe. Unable to contain his own passions, he sought to eliminate them in everyone else. His blinkered view of Mandalorian honor would have reduced the Faithful to mere hirelings, helpless against the Faithless.

And so we did what we had to do: We rejected this deluded Mandalore as thoroughly as we rejected the Anti-Mandalores of the Faithless. Because we were willing to die for our cause, we became the Death Watch, led by the Secret Mandalores. To ensure we would be led by the most powerful, we decreed that any warrior could challenge the Secret Mandalore for leadership of Death Watch. And as our symbol of authority we chose the Darksaber, an ancient weapon liberated from the Jedi long ago.

Jedi antique? Sounds valuable! - Hondo

Tor Vizsla wields the Darksaber, a weapon liberated from the Jedi Order that became the symbol of the Secret Mandalore's authority.

...from your own warped version of it. JANGO

The responsibility of wielding it fell to me.

My first task was to eliminate Mereel and his followers, lest the New Mandalorians exploit our divisions. After many battles, we engineered a trap for them on Korda VI. There I shot Mereel down, erasing him from the history of the Mando'ade. Then, a decade ago, we tricked the Jedi into eliminating the True Mandalorians. We lured the True Mandalorians to Galidraan to put down a pointless insurrection, then brought the Jedi to the same place on the trail of false information. The Jedi slaughtered the True Mandalorians like nerfs on market day, and at last our long struggle was over.

Letting Jedi dupes do the dirty work. Great idea! -Aurra

But even as Mereel's ideas died on Galidraan, Mandalore was in flames. The Great Clan Wars had begun. We declared ourselves and sought to rally our kinsmen to our standard, but we were too few, weakened by petty clan disputes that had flared into conflagrations while the fight with the True Mandalorians distracted us.

The Jedi and True Mandalorians square off on Galidraan.

Meanwhile, centuries of New Mandalorian lies had left the Mando'ade weak and soft. One of my kinswomen, the Duchess Satine Kryze, had been sent offworld as a child by her father, a mighty clan warlord, and she fell prey to the lies of the Jedi. After her father perished in the Great Clan Wars, she betrayed his memory by becoming the leader of the New Mandalorians. Aided by Jedi tricks, she became the newest Anti-Mandalore, whereupon the exhausted Mando'ade flocked to her banner. Some of our warriors were exiled to the moon Concordia. Others—myself included—slipped away to resume the ba'slan shev'la.

Satine is weak-minded, like a child, with a child's faith in goodness and rationality. She has proved all too ready to believe the exiles have given up their fight. In fact, the Death Watch is being rebuilt. As always, our trials have made us stronger.

With the True Mandalorians gone, the Faithful are united again. Satine's people slumber on, begging to be awakened. We shall be the ones to do it. We have backers now, powerful beings who believe in our cause and whom we are using even as they scheme to use us. When we return, it shall be as an army. Our order, professionalism, and honor will be the keys that open the hearts of the Mando'ade.

Death Watch members on a training mission

The Death Watch is thriving under my secret care. Soon the mines of Concordia will rumble with the sound of Mandalorian iron scraped from the rock, and the moon's canyons will fill with warriors clad in beskar'gam. We shall cross the white sands of Mandalore in force, and our people will greet us as liberators. Good luck turning a rabble into an army. - Hondo

I am the Secret Mandalore, defender of our people's honor. I wield the Darksaber, and I shall see Satine overthrown, and her false idols of pacifism and accommodation thrown down. Then the name Mandalorian will inspire fear once again.

This is my burden and my oath.

I made a vow of my own: to kill Tor Vizsla. One of us kept his promise. JANGO

Jango always kept his promises. He was that kind of man - Hondo

BESKAR'GAM (ARMOR)

To outsiders beholding us, our helmets are our faces, just as our suits of armor are our bodies.

The planets and moons of the Mandalore system are rich in beskar, or Mandalorian iron. According to legend, this boon brought the Progenitors to our world. Beskar is enormously strong, able to deflect blaster bolts and even lightsaber blades. Yet it is light and flexible, particularly when forged with carbon and ciridium. A skilled naur'alor can shape beskar into almost any form, manipulating its strength, color, and other properties. This knowledge is ours alone—the penalty for sharing it with outsiders is death.

Good armor. Very strong. (And very expensive.) - Hond

A death sentence from extinct Mandos. How frightening. -Aurr

The Progenitors saw hand-to-hand combat as the warrior's highest calling. Their helmets resembled their own faces, and each suit was custom-made for its wearer, with the armor of venerated ancestors melted down and reforged to equip a particularly valorous war chief or clan leader. Some forged their own armor, while others left that task to metalsmiths serving their clans as vassals.

In battle the Taung Crusaders relied primarily on handheld weapons such as beskade and Mythosaur axes. The beskad is a single-edged, curved sword made of Mandalorian iron and used to batter down enemies' defenses, while the Mythosaur Ax was assembled from calcified plates of mythosaur bone, sharpened and arrayed in a fan shape atop a staff. Crusaders often carried a kal—dagger made of beskar—in their off hand.

Taung weapon forms inspire modern Mandalorian designs.

During the Great Shadow Crusade many Progenitors supplemented their armor with a combat suit hardened against vacuum and supplying several hours' worth of air. After early engagements with the Republic's rocket-jumpers, the Crusaders introduced rocket packs into their arsenal, becoming masters of aerial combat.

The next phase of beskar'gam's evolution came after Mandalore the Ultimate admitted non-Taung to the clans. The look and form of Crusader armor had been shaped by individualism and clan tradition, but now the Mando'ade included many species, united only by adherence to the warrior codes. These newcomers had to be transformed into effective fighting units that could work together against the Republic.

The Fett boy's ancestor? - Hondo

DON'T KNOW. DON'T CARE. BOBA

Cassus Fett's ideas about unit organization reshaped the clans into a potent military machine.

Cassus Fett, Mandalore the Ultimate's chief strategist, forged the clans into an army. After their defeat at the hands of the Republic, some Crusaders had created a new chain of command based not on clan bonds, but on experience and success in warfare. Some found such ideas heretical, but the so-called Neo-Crusaders proved themselves in raids on the Republic borders. Fett persuaded the Ultimate to experiment with their reforms, distributing Neo-Crusader units throughout the ranks of the clans.

The Neo-Crusaders' armor was sleeker and more uniform, though by necessity adapted to fit any number of species. It was also color-coded by rank: blue for rank-and-file troops, silver for front-line units and veterans, red for Rally Masters, and gold for Field Marshals. Most startling to tradition-minded Mandalorians, it was rarely made of beskar. There was no way to mine and forge beskar quickly enough to outfit the greatly expanded Mandalorian force.

The Mando'ade have yet to field a fighting force as potent or organized as that destroyed at Ani'la Akaan. During the long centuries of the Stagnation, Mandalorians returned to the individualism of the Crusaders' time, combining pieces of inherited, repurposed, scavenged, and stolen armor. Mandalore

The color-coded ranks of the Neo-Crusaders: regular troops (blue), field marshals (gold), rally masters (red), and front-line troops/veteran units (silver)

the Uniter restarted the mass production of beskar'gam, but Mandalorians' personal preferences continued to determine their choice of weapons and armor, and thus their battle styles, techniques, and strengths.

But while allowing for such individuality, the Uniter created a new order of shocktroopers more mobile than the Neo-Crusaders—warriors who would rely on speed and surprise in making their attacks.

The armor of the Uniter's shocktroopers was stripped down and light, so as not to overburden a jetpack's fuel supplies. A liner shirt with a micro energy-field projector and two layers of ceramic plating offered basic protection for the torso. Next came a flight suit to protect against everything from water to hard vacuum, stiffened with beskar armorweave. Atop that were plates of beskar or duraplast, designed to protect vital organs. Special units wore kamas to protect against shrapnel, blast damage, and jetpack wash. The Uniter's armor remains the basis for that worn by the Faithful today.

No two Watchers are the same, and any warrior is free to customize his or her armor to best fit responsibilities and fighting styles. But to modify armor effectively, one must first understand the basics of beskar'gam.

Many armor components are paired. The right piece is known as the beskad, while the left piece is the kal. This terminology holds even for warriors who favor their left hands.

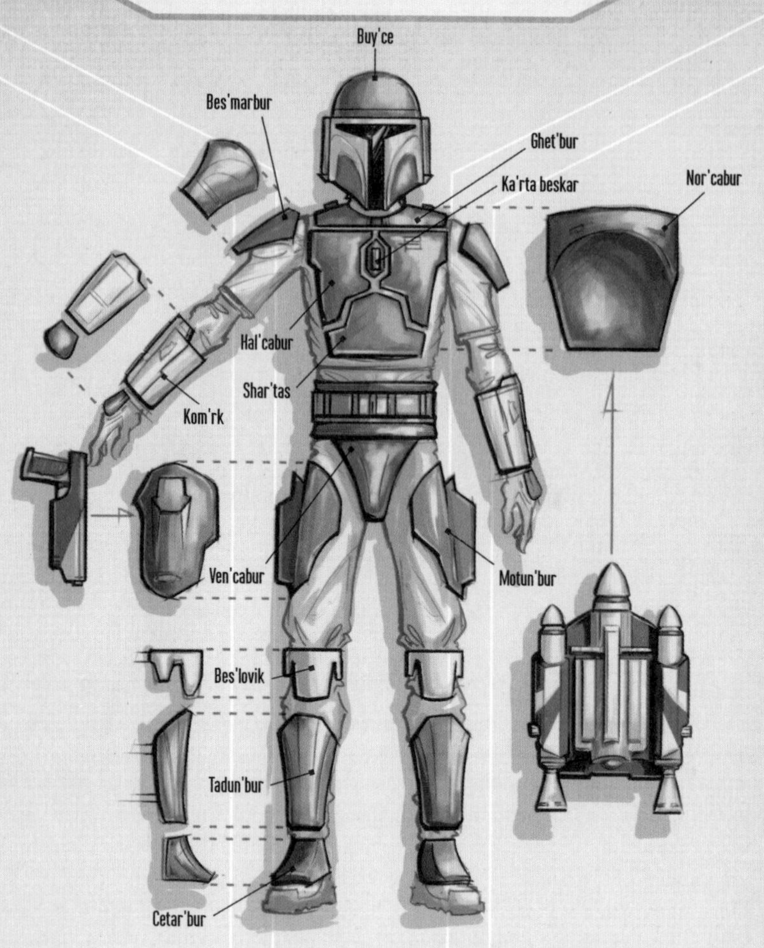

The buy'ce (barbute or helmet) is both a symbol of the Mando'ade and the most important piece of one's kit (see separate entry on Death Watch helmets).

The haalas (cuirass) protects the torso and consists of five components. The main pieces are the beskad and kal hal'cabure, or breastplates. At the juncture of the breastplates sits a small lozenge-shaped piece of armor known as the ka'rta beskar or tapul. Beneath the breastplates is the shar'tas, or placard, which protects a humanoid's stomach and innards. Above the breastplates is the ghet'bur, or gorget, protecting the upper chest. Earlier Mandalorian armor included a jatne ghet'bur, or upper gorget, which protected the throat, but it could hinder free movement and so is rarely used today. The gorget attaches to the nor'cabur, or backplate, which is reinforced to help bear the weight of the jetpack.

IF YOU'RE HUNTING JEDI, WEAR THAT UPPER GORGET. IF ONLY MY FATHER HAD. BOBA

The bes'marbure, or spaulders, protect the shoulders, and are reduced in size from the pauldrons of ancient Mandalorian armor. The kal spaulder is for unit insignia; clan or personal marks go on the beskad spaulder.

Ancient Mandalorian armor included shun'bure, or rerebraces to protect the biceps, but these have been dropped from modern armor. The kom'rks (vambraces or gauntlets) protecting the forearms remain, though primarily as weapon mounts. Note that left-handed Death Watch members often mount their weapons in reverse, a factor that strategists must take into account when planning unit actions.

Don't add ever weapon yo have to y gauntlets. Select th right weapons f the missio
JANG

The groin is protected by the ven'cabur, or codpiece. Some warriors wear a corresponding back piece, the hut'uun cabur, or culet.

The thighs are protected by motun'bure, or cuissards, which vary in form. Some warriors favor full cuissards that protect the back and front of the thighs, while others opt for front protection only. Other warriors omit cuissards altogether.

The knees are protected by the bes'lovike (poleyns), which offer both protection and a site for mounting additional weapons.

The shins and calves are protected by tadun'bure (greaves) though most warriors dispense with rear greaves. The cetar'bure (sabatons) protect the tops of the feet.

Interesting. - Hondo

Our secret mining operations on Mandalore and Concordia are producing more and more beskar, but Mandalorian armor remains hard to find—and the New Mandalorians treacherously destroyed many heirloom suits of beskar'gam. Most of our modern armor is forged from duraplast or alum.

Traditionally, warriors have decorated their armor with clan colors and insignia, inscribed it with sigils celebrating victories, painted it in recognition of goals or causes, or customized it in other ways. The Death Watch honors these traditions, but for now our highest priority is to appear as a single united, disciplined military force. Until our fight becomes our people's fight, therefore, our standard uniform shall be polished beskar'gam with blue accents, the color signifying our devotion.

It's hard to believe these criminals will now wear armor that looks like mine. Still, confusion to be exploited. Always look for an advantage.
JANGO

The Taung prove their valor against a mythosaur on ancient Mandalore.

SYMBOLS AND UNIT INSIGNIAS

MYTHOSAUR SKULL: When the Progenitors arrived, Mandalore was inhabited by huge horned creatures—the savage mythosaurs. The clans tested themselves in battle against these great beasts, until all had fallen before their axes and swords. The mask of Mandalore the First was made from the ridged sternum over the mythosaur's heart, and during the Great Shadow Crusade the image of the massive skull was the sigil of Clan Keldau, famed for its combat trainers. Both mythosaurs and Clan Keldau are long gone, but the skull sigil remains a common symbol of the Mando'ade.

CRUSADER LOGO: The ancient symbol of the Mandalorian Crusaders is a ring adorned with sharp points. The points represent the weapons of warriors, while the ring symbolizes the cycles that govern life—birth and death, conquest and defeat, and the promise that new warriors will arise to carry on the traditions of the departed.

NEO-CRUSADER LOGO: Said to be the invention of Cassus Fett, the logo of the Neo-Crusaders pairs the symbol of their Crusader forebears with a stylized Mandalorian skull, symbolizing the authority of the Mandalore to interpret the will of the war gods.

JAIG EYES: No sound is more terrifying to the creatures of the Mandalorian night than the piercing cry of the jai'galaar, the shriek-hawk. Shriek-hawks are peerless hunters, but never more dangerous than when defending their nests. The stylized eyes of the shriek-hawk are awarded to warriors showing conspicuous bravery in defense of their clan or unit, or of Mandalorians in general.

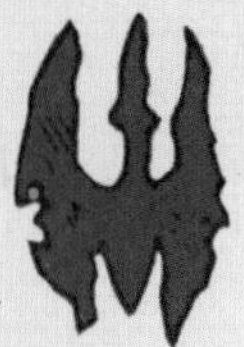

DEATH WATCH: Upon becoming the leader of Death Watch, I chose the sigil of my own clan to represent it. Why? Because our clan symbol represents the shriek-hawk in threat display, a noble Mandalorian symbol if ever there was one. And because if we are to reclaim our honor, clans such as my own must decide where their loyalties lie. When Vizslas see their own sigil adorning the armor of those fighting for the ancient warrior ways, perhaps they will remember their own lost honor.

This was Jaster Mereel's sigil as a journeyman protector on Concord Dawn. I displayed to honor him and to remind myself th you never know the heart of another. Alw assume betrayal is just a moment awa You'll live longer. JANGO

THE HELMET

The modern Mandalorian helmet is a technological marvel, one that allows a well-trained Watcher to see in all directions, communicate easily, and fight more effectively than a dozen common soldiers.

The helmet's viewplate automatically augments vision in low-light conditions and protects it from peaks in intensity, preventing a Watcher from being blinded by explosions or luma-weapons. The viewplate's macrobinocular

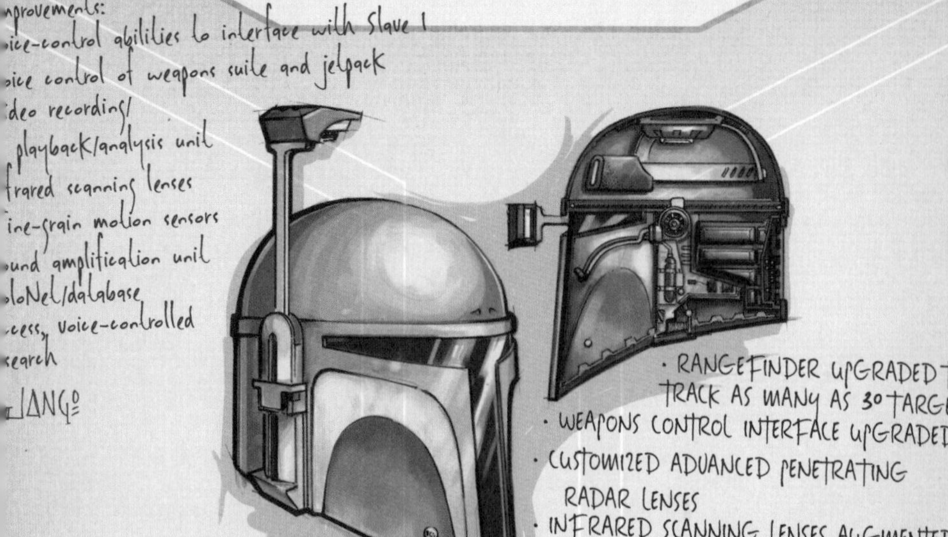

A modern Mandalorian helmet

lenses interface with the rangefinder, selecting as many as 10 targets for tracking via the heads-up display, controlled either by voice commands or eye movements and blinking. A pineal sensor and microcameras let the wearer see behind him. An encrypted internal comlink allows communications with other Watchers, while a broadband antenna is included for longer-range transmissions. The helmet has a two-hour reserve air tank and an environmental filter to eliminate contaminants. *So that's how they do it. -Aurra*

Now this is a good trick! - Hond

THE JETPACK

To fulfill mission objectives as quickly as possible, a Watcher must strike with speed and decisive force, and engage targets with surgical precision. Our aerial assault capabilities give us something critical our opponents lack. We can attack targets all across Mandalore and on Republic worlds, appearing and disappearing while our adversaries are still trying to take stock of the damage we've caused. Our jetpacks are the key to this capability.

In ancient times Mandalorian Crusaders and shocktroopers were the pride of the Mando'ade, swooping down without warning. Every sighting of Watchers racing across the sky in formation is a reminder of what has been taken from us by the Anti-Mandalores and their conspirators among the Jedi and the

Republic. Jetpack units, organized along the same lines as armadas of starfighters or gunships—with flight leaders, clear mission objectives, constant communication, linked fields of fire, and well-defined coverage responsibilities—are magnificent examples of skill, training, and precision.

Great for quick getaways, but murder on the spine. -Aurra

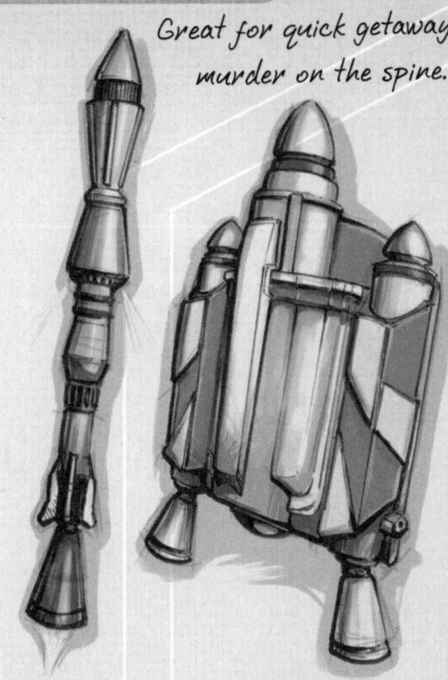

Mitrinomon's Z-6 fine-bore missile (left) and a Merr-Sonn JT-12 jetpack

The jetpack is simultaneously a means of propulsion and a valuable weapon. A Watcher must master both aspects of its use.

The standard model used by the Death Watch is the Merr-Sonn JT-12, a compact, lightweight jetpack with fuel for one minute of continuous operation. It's possible to carry additional fuel bladders, but this increases weight. We are working with sympathizers within Merr-Sonn and at other corporations to find light, solid-state fuel that will increase our packs' versatility.

The JT-12's standard armament is a missile launcher carrying a single concussion warhead. Because the missile thrust vent is located on the bottom of the jetpack, some Death Watchmen wear kamas for protection against the exhaust. The JT-12 launcher can carry a variety of missiles. The Z-6 fine-bore missile from Mitrinomon, which can be set to explode upon impact or be locked "dead" and used as a grappling hook, is a popular choice.

A JETPACK LETS YOU DISGUISE A CHANGE OF POSITION AS A FALL AND REGAIN THE ADVANTAGE. PLUS AT TOP VELOCITY, YOU YOURSELF BECOME A WEAPON. BOBA

RECRUITING

We cannot openly recruit and train personnel. As the New Mandalorians consider us outlaws to be exiled or disarmed, we must beware of double agents whose true allegiance lies with the New Mandalorians, the remnants of the True Mandalorians, the Republic, the Hutts, or others.

Therefore we are ever-vigilant about those we adopt into our ranks, constantly supervising and rigorously testing recruits and even experienced Watchers.

Never get shot at unless someone's paying. -Aurra

Should you suspect a recruit or a fellow Death Watchman of divided loyalties or treason, inform your commanding officer, who will assist you in following our protocols: spot, monitor, isolate, interrogate. Do not fear the effect on your relationship with an individual soldier. If Watchers lose focus when interrogated by their peers during a mere training exercise, how will they react when under fire by our enemies? The honorable do not fear questions, just as the worthy do not fear testing.

Where do we find potential Watchers? Many places:

CLAN: Every clan has been divided between supporters of the Faithful and adherents of the Faithless since the Annihilation, and rivalries among clans have existed for far longer than that.

Death Watch is a secret affiliation, not to be shared with kin and clan. But we also know that the clans are ideal recruiting grounds. To balance the benefits of clan recruitment against the dangers of exposure, three Watchers must endorse a potential recruit found through clan ties, and one of those Watchers must be from a different clan.

INDUSTRY: The New Mandalorians have channeled our people's spirit and ingenuity into making ships, vehicles, and equipment for outsiders. But within every Mandalorian corporation we find frustrated artisans and creators who know their talents are being wasted, and who yearn for an opportunity to harness them in service of our cause. Why else would MandalMotors and MandalTech models prove so readily adaptable to military uses?

We have spotters in Mandalorian companies who watch for potential Death Watch recruits. These spotters never make contact directly—they are too valuable to risk exposing. Rather, they contact another Watcher about a potential recruit, and that Watcher contacts a third, who is tasked with the actual recruiting effort.

Too much work! I'll stick to pirating. - Hondo

LAW ENFORCEMENT: Mandalore's police and emergency services are part of the Mandalorian Guard and attract Mando'ade who want to protect their people. This makes them logical sources of recruitment. Such recruits come to Death Watch with substantial training in arms and working as part of a unit. At the same time, we must be mindful that the New Mandalorian government closely monitors the Mandalorian Guard, particularly its elite units. Recruits from these units are valuable, but must be carefully screened. As with our industry efforts, we maintain a system of spotters and recruiters and carefully maintain distance between the two.

MANDALORIAN WORLDS/ENCLAVES: The Mando'ade are spread across the worlds of Mandalorian Space, and enclaves of our people exist across the galaxy. These populations offer great potential for filling the ranks of the Death Watch. Remember that some of the greatest Mandalores were born or grew up far from our homeworld. Mandalore the Binder was born the son of a rug weaver on Harswee, while Mandalore the Hammerborn grew up in the alleys of Kol Atorn, learning accented Mando'a from the emigrants and exiles who had settled there.

Mandalore the Binder

MERCENARIES/BOUNTY HUNTERS: Many veteran Watchers have served as mercs or bounty hunters, and experienced fighters are an obvious help to us. But not every Mandalorian merc is a proper recruit. Some are Mandalorians in name only, trading on our reputation and appearance without embracing the Six Actions. And while there is no dishonor in mercenary service or the Crimson Trade, those who work for the highest bidder may change sides for a few credits more.

Not for a few more credits. - Hondo

These recruits are carefully screened and watched during training. We welcome those who are willing to put aside their old ways, and we quickly part company with those who are not.

Finally, a note on outsiders. Yes, any warriors who prove themselves in battle and follow the Six Actions may become Mando'ade. Our society is based on actions and achievement, not on birth or background. This creed has kept our society strong for millennia.

But these are not typical times. The Mando'ade have been divided and lied to, lured away from their heritage by the Faithless and their laandur Duchess. We cannot defeat her on the battlefield just yet. Instead, our victories must come on more private territory: the hearts and minds of the Mando'ade. For that

Some mercs use the Six Actions as a cloak for their own violence. JANGO reason, we must look like a uniform fighting force, with similar helmets and human faces beneath them. When we restore our traditions, perhaps we will welcome outsiders once again. But until then, we are at war. Incorporating beast species undermines security and works against the image we must project.

Ha! I wouldn't want to be a member of this crazy club anyway. - Hondo

TRAINING

Death Watch recruits go through four weeks of basic training, learning not only the basic skills of combat but also the fundamentals of operating within a military unit. Even experienced soldiers go through basic training; weeding out the unworthy or poorly motivated is as important as the teaching process. By the end of basic training, recruits will have learned to accept authority and be able to perform basic combat maneuvers automatically, even when disoriented or exhausted. Such training will pay off in lives saved and mission objectives accomplished.

Typically, we train recruits in squads of 10, each squad divided into two fire teams. Rally Masters serve as drill sergeants for the duration of basic training, which takes place in one of our secure locations. For operational security, recruits are never told where they're going.

Wise. When working with others, reveal only what they need to know. -Aurra

A Death Watch training squad under the watchful eye of its Rally Master

After basic training, the remaining recruits are reorganized into fire teams and squads; physical training continues for another two to four weeks, though the emphasis shifts to ranged and melee weapons and then to unarmed combat techniques. Recruits who complete this stage learn tactics as well as Mandalorian history and Death Watch objectives. This stage of training culminates in live-fire drills and war games.

The fourth and final stage of training takes two weeks and focuses primarily on jetpack operation, maneuvers, and tactics. Once jetpack training is complete, the recruits take the oath of the Death Watch and don their beskar'gam.

Jetpack training is the final stage before recruits take the Death Watch oath.

OPERATION PROFILES

Our struggle against the New Mandalorians will not end with the capture of a fortress or city. We must be flexible and opportunistic, seizing moments when they present themselves and constantly reassessing situations and changing the strategies that address them.

Regardless of the operation, we are never captured, never leave dead or wounded behind, and never abandon equipment if it can be helped. There are multiple reasons for this:

- We don't want our adversaries to know about our equipment, tactics, or membership.

- We are more effective when rumors and misinformation increase our perceived numbers and decrease our perceived casualties.
- We are Mando'ade—better to die than live in dishonor.

Nonsense! Rule No. 1 is Stay alive. - Hondo-

These are the six common operation profiles every Watcher must be prepared to carry out with minimal notice:

RECON: Soldiers need information as much as bravery and training. Recon missions teach us about our enemies' strengths, weaknesses, movements, and positions. Recon missions can make use of informers and sympathetic civilians and benefit from slicing into data networks or satellite feeds, but there's no substitute for a soldier's firsthand assessment of the situation on the ground.

Good advice. Only believe your own eyes. —Aurra

RAID: The simplest operations involve getting in, eliminating opposition, fulfilling mission objectives, and getting out. Objectives can vary, from inflicting casualties or destroying matériel to gaining information and equipment, but the tactic is always to get in and out with lightning speed.

AMBUSH: The combination of well-trained soldiers and a chokepoint in terrain or construction is a natural force multiplier. There is nothing dishonorable about ambush tactics. Making the best use of the battlefield and one's resources is a tactic as old as war itself.

Death Watch warriors gathering intelligence for a successful strike

STRIKE: The difference between a raid and a strike is that the objective of a strike is a game-changer: the elimination of a key individual, the destruction of a complex, or the seizure of key equipment or intelligence. Strikes are more carefully planned than raids, and often require multiple fire teams or squads acting in concert.

INFILTRATION: Infiltration operations can be a precursor to a raid or strike, with Death Watchmen penetrating enemy security and remaining in place to support our forces. Such operations may require the cooperation of informers and sympathizers and may be conducted out of uniform. To avoid losing assets to friendly fire, recognition signals must be established for use during infiltration activities.

DESTABILIZATION: Lacking the numbers or resources to oppose the Faithless in conventional warfare, we undermine them by demonstrating that they are unfit to rule Mandalore and cannot guarantee safety and security. Destabilization can take many forms—propaganda inserted into New Mandalorian datafeeds, public attacks on New Mandalorian targets, destruction of symbols of the regime, and so forth. Destabilization operations rely on clear objectives: What do we seek to accomplish, and will this accomplishment improve the perception of Death Watch while diminishing that of the New Mandalorians? An ill-advised destabilization operation does our cause more damage than good.

INTRODUCTION TO TACTICS

Operational profiles vary, but general principles always apply. Follow these principles and your operations have a better chance of success. Neglect them, and failure is all but certain.

REDUNDANCY: Things go wrong. Soldiers are unfit for duty or get lost, equipment malfunctions, batteries fail, weather conditions turn. A wise commander plans for contingencies.

ECONOMY: Committing all available assets to a single mission is dangerous. Soldiers can get in one another's way, and ill fortune can be devastating. Figure out the optimum force for fulfilling a mission objective, and keep additional units in reserve or use them to bolster the main force elsewhere.

CLARITY: Soldiers must understand their mission objectives, tactics, and chain of command. Drill them until their responses are as close to automatic as possible. A well-trained unit can see through the fog of war because it has encountered problems in simulations and learned to apply solutions.

FOCUS: Do not waver from the mission objective. Time and resources are precious in battle; use them for their intended purposes.

FLEXIBILITY: The mission objective is paramount, but there may be different ways to achieve it. Commanders should be alert for unexpected opportunities.

INITIATIVE: Opportunities come to the commander with a history of seizing them, and Death Watch acts where the New Mandalorians merely react. Do not surrender this advantage.

MOBILITY: Keep moving. Small forces need surprise, speed, and skill to prevent larger forces from bringing their numerical and resource advantages to bear. Get pinned down and advantages quickly turn into disadvantages.

SECURITY: Soldiers who talk endanger the mission and the lives of fellow Watchers. Be particularly careful if a mission involves informers or sympathizers. Consider using a second informer or sympathizer as a spotter to look for breaches of operational security, and deal immediately and harshly with any loose talk within a Death Watch unit.

Never leave witnesses. -Aurra

BUT LEAVING ALLIES IS FINE. RIGHT, AURRA? BOBA

PURPOSE: We are the Death Watch, the standard bearers of Mandalorian destiny. Our enemies are the misguided architects of a weak and flawed new order, one that cannot stand. This alone will not guarantee victory, but it is an advantage that will see a resolute heart through many difficulties.

KNOW YOUR ENEMIES

Many in the galaxy detest the idea of a renewed, ascendant Mandalore whose people are united by pride in their common heritage. In combating our enemies, though, we must distinguish between the gebaru'e and the chaajaru'e—the near and far enemies.

The bulk of the gebaru'e are the forces of the New Mandalorians, pursuing Duchess Satine's misguided program of pacifism. Some among these Faithless actively seek our destruction. They will die, either when we invade or later, when interrogations reveal who was faithful and who was not. But others among the gebaru'e are reluctant combatants at best. It is from their ranks that the Death Watch will grow and draw strength.

Imagine the fun if I were to sell this book to the Duchess. -Aurra

In determining mission objectives, we should consider the impact on the gebaru'e. Sometimes a show of disciplined, carefully calibrated force will gain us more than an extravagant display of that force.

Most of the chaajaru'e are the forces of the Republic, our ancient enemies. The Republic is decadent and dissipated, a great beast whose death throes threaten to crush the free peoples of the galaxy. The chaajaru'e have overwhelming advantages in resources and technology, which we must remember in seeking to thwart their plots. One day our sacrifices will create a Mandalore powerful enough to challenge the chaajaru'e openly. But this will be the work of our children and our children's children. As members of Death Watch, we must be not just brave but also patient.

THE MANDALORIAN GUARD: The Mandalorian Guard includes law-enforcement and public-safety units. It also inlcudes operating authorities throughout the sector.

After the Great Clan Wars, Satine reorganized the Guard, whose units had become power bases for the clans. Guard units are now typically drawn from multiple clans, with promotions and chains of command engineered to break up clan concentrations. This has bred resentment as veteran Guardsmen see promotions go to less-qualified members of other clans, rather than to deserving members of their own. Those passed over are potential Death Watch recruits, but they must understand that we also demand the subordination of clan loyalties to a larger cause.

Mandalorian Guard units vary greatly in ability and loyalty to the New Mandalorians.

Most Guardsmen wear body armor and use stun batons and shields. They train with blasters, flamethrowers, and heavy weapons, but they use them only as a last resort. Elite units, such as the Mandalorian Secret Service, have trained with jetpacks and are formidable opponents.

MANDALORIAN ROYAL GUARD: This unit defends Duchess Satine and her top-ranking ministers. While an elite unit, the Royal Guard contains few truly superior warriors. Duchess Satine abhors violence, and insists that her protectors use great restraint in their duties. We have tried to infiltrate the Royal Guard, but the Duchess has so far chosen wisely in filling its ranks, and our efforts have come to naught.

Royal Guardsmen are typically armed with electrostaffs, and they fight in concert effectively. We suspect they have heavier weapons as well, but have no credible reports that they have used them.

MANDALORIAN PATROL: These Guard units defend Mandalorian Space. They are more aggressive than regular Guardsmen, intercepting smugglers and suspicious craft with deadly force, if required. Beyond a handful of heavy cruisers, the Patrol has few capital ships, relying on small, speedy patrol craft backed up by corvettes and frigates.

Don't mess with these guys. It's not worth it. -Aurra

Where possible, avoid Patrolmen. They are more concerned with criminals and the kunaru'a than with us. The Patrol contains many Death Watch sympathizers, and in recent years we have had little trouble learning of routes and maneuvers in advance, allowing us to keep out of each other's way.

TRUE MANDALORIAN REMNANTS: Though we vanquished the True Mandalorians at Galidraan, their creed is not yet extinct. We must remember that those True Mandalorians who escaped Galidraan are as familiar with the ba'slan shev'la as we are. Be watchful for signs that they—or others espousing their goals—have reorganized.

THE REPUBLIC MILITARY: Nearly a millennium ago the Republic largely abandoned its standing military, ceding responsibility for most security to local Planetary Security Forces such as the Mandalorian Patrol. The Republic's lone centrally controlled military organization is the small group of task forces and fleets known as the Judicial Forces. While limited in capabilities, the Judicials can requisition military units from sectors and star systems during times of crisis, and their rapid-response fleets are designed to respond to trouble anywhere in the galaxy.

The Judicials have been weakened by political strife and corruption, and the galaxy's best warship crews (as well as some of the worst) are found among the Planetary Security Forces. These forces' capabilities and resources vary widely; to conduct a successful mission outside Mandalorian Space, it is essential to know the composition, routines, and protocols of local forces.

We must also keep careful watch on Republic politics. Recent incidents have energized a political movement to restore the Republic's centralized military capabilities. A force created by such actions would be far stronger than the Judicials and presumably less hampered by bureaucracy.

JEDI AND SITH: These sorcerers have interfered in our affairs for millennia. The ancient Jedi demolished Mandalore the Ultimate's empire and broke our clans at Ani'la Akaan, and their descendants oversaw the Annihilation. Today, Jedi agents work in secret to thwart our aims. The Sith are no better, having repeatedly beguiled the Mando'ade into serving as their shock troops.

Do not underestimate Jedi powers. Most Jedi are superb warriors with heightened senses and reflexes. Jedi lightsabers can redirect blaster bolts; to counter this, maintain sufficient distance so that you have a better chance to react to reflected bolts, and do not fire unnecessarily. A better tactic is to use your flamethrower. Jedi powers and weapons are far less effective against attacks that cover a large area.

The aftermath of a successful swarm offense against a Jedi Knight

Jedi pinned by a fibercord launcher. Nice. -Aurra

Another effective tactic is to pin Jedi using your fibercord launcher. This is best done as a group—a valuable strategy in all combat with Jedi. They are dangerous opponents, but not even their powers allow them to escape dozens of bolts, overlapping fields of flame, or multiple grapples.

Remember that Jedi powers are not limited to the battlefield. They can manipulate objects and devices, and they use their abilities to confuse the unwary, erase memories, and even implant suggestions. The strong-minded can resist these powers, but this takes training and dedication. If a Jedi or Sith is in the area, Rally Masters should note strange incidents, peculiar behavior, or other unexpected phenomena. These may be evidence of Jedi sorcery at work.

CONCLUSION

We live in an era in which we are beset by enemies and stand in danger of seeing our very heritage and history expunged by the most insidious foes of all—our own people.

Yet the Mando'ade have always been tested, subjected to trials by both the weak who stand among us and the strong who stand apart from us. Both seek our destruction, but neither will succeed. For we are strengthened by many things: skill at arms and the craft of war, toughness of mind and clarity of vision, and faith in the ancient values that have preserved us.

By studying this manual, you become a more resolute leader. By learning other Death Watch lore, you become a more effective teacher. By subjecting yourself to trials, you become a more capable warrior. Every lesson and every victory brings us closer to the triumph of our cause and the resurgence of our people.

Learn YOUR OWN lessons. Define YOUR OWN victories.
-Aurra

Yes! Yes! Stay alive. Get rich - Hondo

Every resolute warrior brings the glorious future of Mandalore closer to reality.

Library of Congress Cataloging-in-Publication Data available.
ISBN: 978-1-4521-3321-8

Star Wars: The Bounty Hunter Code is produced by becker&mayer!
11120 NE 33rd Place, Suite 101
Bellevue, Washington 98004
www.beckermayer.com

If you have questions or comments about this product, please visit www.beckermayer.com/customerservice.html and click on Customer Service Request Form.

Editor: Ben Grossblatt
Designer: Rosanna Brockley
Production coordinator: Jennifer Marx
Design assistance: Greg Cook

Lucasfilm Ltd.
Executive Editor: J. W. Rinzler
Art Director: Troy Alders
Keeper of the Holocron: Leland Chee
Director of Publishing: Carol Roeder

www.starwars.com

10 9 8 7 6 5 4 3

Manufactured in China

Text and annotations written by Daniel Wallace, Ryder Windham, and Jason Fry.

Illustrations by Alan Brooks, Joe Corroney, Mark McHaley, Gustavo Mendonca, Chris Reiff, Brian Rood, Chris Scalf, Chris Trevas, John Van Fleet, and Velvet Engine Pte Ltd.

Chronicle Books LLC
680 Second Street
San Francisco, California 94107

www.chroniclebooks.com